"So, how would we do this, then? I mean, how could you watch over me, go after whoever this is, do whatever you need to do, without people knowing?"

Falco had considered that during the six-hour flight from New York. There were lots of ways to move into someone's life to provide protection and search out information without raising questions. The idea was to assume a role other people would accept. He could pass himself off as her driver. Her assistant. Her personal trainer.

Okay. Personal trainer it would be…

"Mr. Orsini?"

"Falco," he said, looking down into her eyes. He saw the rise and fall of her breasts, remembered the soft, lush feel of her against him, and he knew damned well he wasn't going to pretend to be her trainer after all.

"Simple," he said calmly. "We'll make people think I'm your lover."

She stared at him. Then she gave a little laugh.

"That's crazy," she said. "No one will believe—"

"Yeah," he said, his voice low and rough. "Yeah, they will."

Falco reached out, gathered Elle in his arms, and kissed her.

The patriarch of a powerful Sicilian dynasty,
Cesare Orsini has fallen ill, and he wants
atonement before he dies.

One by one he sends for his sons—
he has a mission for each to help him
clear his conscience.

His sons are proud and determined,
but they will do their duty—the tasks they
undertake will change their lives forever!
They are…

*Darkly handsome—proud and arrogant
The perfect Sicilian husbands!*

by

Sandra Marton

*Raffaele: Taming His Tempestuous Virgin
Dante: Claiming His Secret Love-Child
Falco: The Dark Guardian*

Coming next month:

Nicolo: The Powerful Sicilian
December 2010

Sandra Marton

FALCO: THE DARK GUARDIAN

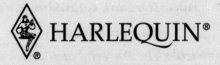

TORONTO • NEW YORK • LONDON
AMSTERDAM • PARIS • SYDNEY • HAMBURG
STOCKHOLM • ATHENS • TOKYO • MILAN • MADRID
PRAGUE • WARSAW • BUDAPEST • AUCKLAND

Recycling programs
for this product may
not exist in your area.

ISBN-13: 978-0-373-12953-9

FALCO: THE DARK GUARDIAN

First North American Publication 2010.

Copyright © 2010 by Sandra Myles.

www.eHarlequin.com

Printed in U.S.A.

All about the author...
Sandra Marton

SANDRA MARTON wrote her first novel while she
was still in elementary school. Her doting parents told
her she'd be a writer someday and Sandra believed
them. In high school and college, she wrote dark
poetry nobody but her boyfriend understood, though
looking back, she suspects he was just being kind.
As a wife and mother, she wrote murky short stories
in what little spare time she could manage, but not
even her boyfriend-turned-husband could pretend
to understand those. Sandra tried her hand at other
things, among them teaching and serving on the board
of education in her hometown, but the dream of
becoming a writer was always in her heart.

At last Sandra realized she wanted to write books
about what all women hope to find: love with that
one special man, love that's rich with fire and passion,
love that lasts forever. She wrote a novel, her very
first, and sold it to the Harlequin® Presents line. Since
then, she's written more than seventy books, all of
them featuring sexy, gorgeous, larger-than-life heroes.
A four-time RITA® Award finalist, she's also received
eight *RT Book Reviews* awards for Best Harlequin®
Presents of the Year and has been honored with an
RT Book Reviews Career Achievement Award for
Series Romance. Sandra lives with her very own sexy,
gorgeous, larger-than-life hero in a sun-filled house on
a quiet country lane in the northeastern United States.

Sandra loves to hear from her readers. You can contact
her through her Web site, www.sandramarton.com, or
at P.O. Box 295, Storrs, CT 06268.

CHAPTER ONE

THERE were those who said that Falco Orsini was too rich, too good-looking, too arrogant for his own good.

Falco would have agreed that he was rich, that he was probably arrogant, and if you judged his looks by the seemingly endless stream of beautiful women who moved in and out of his bed, well, he'd have had to admit that perhaps he had something going for him that women liked.

There were also those who called him heartless. He would not have agreed with that.

He was not heartless. He was honest. Why let a competitor buy an elite investment bank if he could scoop it up instead? Why let a competitor get the edge in a business deal if he could get it first? Why go on pretending interest in a woman when he no longer felt any?

It wasn't as if he was a man who ever made promises he had no intention of keeping.

Honest, not heartless. And in the prime of life.

Falco was, like his three brothers, tall. Six foot three. Hard of face, hard of body. Buff, women said. That was true but it had nothing to do with vanity. He was fit the way a man must be when he knows keeping himself that way could mean the difference between life and death.

Not that he lived that kind of existence anymore.

Not often, at any rate.

Not that he talked about.

At thirty-two, Falco had already led what many would consider an interesting life.

At eighteen, he'd grabbed his backpack and thumbed his way around the world. At nineteen, he'd joined the army. At twenty, he became a Special Forces warrior. Someplace along the way, he picked up a bunch of disparate university credits, a skill at high-stakes gambling and, eventually, a passion for high-stakes investing.

He lived by his own rules. He always had. The opinions of others didn't concern him. He believed in honor, duty and integrity. Men who'd served with him, men who dealt with him, didn't always like him—he was too removed, some said—but they respected him almost as much as women coveted him.

Or hated him.

It didn't matter.

Family was everything.

He loved his brothers the same way they loved him, with a ferocity that made the four of them as formidable in everything as they were in business. He would have given his life for his sisters, who would happily have returned the favor. He adored his mother, who worshipped all her sons as perhaps only Italian mothers can.

His father…

Who gave a damn about him?

Falco, like his brothers, had written off Cesare Orsini years ago. As far as his wife and daughters were concerned, Cesare owned a carting company, a construction firm and some of New York City's priciest real estate.

His sons knew the truth.

Their father was the head of something he referred to only as La Famigilia.

He was, in other words, the same as the thugs who had originated in Sicily in the last half of the nineteenth century. Nothing could change that, not the Brioni suits, not the enormous mansion in what had once been Manhattan's Little Italy and was now Greenwich Village. But, for their mother's sake, there were times Falco and his brothers put that aside and pretended the Orsinis were just another big, happy Sicilian-American family.

Today, for instance. On this bright, late autumn afternoon, Dante had taken a wife.

Falco still had trouble getting his head around that.

First Rafe. Now Dante. Two brothers with wives. And, Dante, it turned out, wasn't just a husband, he was also a father.

Nicolo and Falco had spent the day smiling, kissing their new sisters-in-law and grinning at Dante and Rafe. They'd done their best not to feel like jerks cooing at their infant nephew—not that it was difficult because the kid was clearly the world's cutest, most intelligent baby. They'd danced with their sisters and shut their ears to Anna's and Isabella's not-so-subtle hints that they had friends who'd make them perfect wives.

By late afternoon, they were more than ready to slip away and toast their bachelorhood with a few well-earned cold beers at a place the four brothers owned. Not their investment firm. This place was called, simply enough, The Bar.

Cesare headed them off before they could get to the door. He wanted to talk to them, he said.

Not again, Falco had thought wearily. One look at Nick's face and he knew his brother was thinking the same thing. For months now, the Don had been giving his "after I'm dead" speech. The combination to his safe. The names of his attorney and his accountant. The location of important papers. Stuff none of the brothers cared about; none of them wanted a penny of their father's money.

Falco's initial instinct was to ignore Cesare and keep walking.

Instead, he and Nick looked at each other. Maybe the long day had put them in a mellow mood. Maybe it was the champagne. What the hell, Nick's expression said, and Falco replied with a sigh that clearly said, Yeah, why not.

Their father had insisted on talking to them separately. Felipe, Cesare's capo, jerked his head, indicating Falco should go first.

Falco gave a moment's thought to grabbing the capo by his skinny neck, hoisting him to his toes and telling him what a slimy bastard he was to have spent his life as the Don's guard dog, but the family celebration was still going strong in the conservatory at the rear of the house.

So he smiled instead, the kind of smile a man like the capo would surely understand, moved past him and entered Cesare's study. Felipe shut the door behind him....

And Falco found himself in an endurance contest.

His father, seated at his desk, the heavy drapes behind him drawn so that the big room with its oversized furniture seemed even more gloomy than usual, looked up, nodded, waved a manicured hand toward a chair—a gesture Falco ignored—and went back to leafing through the contents of a manila folder.

According to the antique mahogany clock that hung on a wall, all but lost among photos of politicians, old-country ancestors and age-yellowed religious paintings, four minutes ticked away.

Falco stood perfectly still, feet slightly apart, arms folded, dark eyes locked on the clock. The minute hand ticked to yet another marker, the hour hand made its barely perceptible jump. Falco unfolded his arms, turned his back on his father and went to the door.

"Where are you going?"

Falco didn't bother turning around. "*Ciao,* Father. As always, it's been a pleasure."

The chair creaked. Falco knew the Don was pushing back from his desk.

"We have not yet had our talk."

"Our talk? You were the one who requested this meeting." Falco swung toward his father. "If you have something to say, say it—but I assure you, I recall your touching words the last time I saw you. Perhaps you don't remember my response so let me remind you of it. I don't give a damn about your safe, your documents, your business interests—"

"Then you are a fool," the Don said mildly. "Those things are worth a fortune."

A cool smile lifted the corners of Falco's mouth. "So am I, in case you hadn't noticed." His smile vanished. "Even if I weren't, I wouldn't touch anything of yours. You should know that by now."

"Such drama, my son."

"*Questa verità*, Father. Such truth, you mean."

Cesare sighed. "All right. You've made your speech."

"And you've made yours. Goodbye, Father. I'll tell Nicolo to—"

"What were you doing in Athens last month?"

Falco stood absolutely still. "What?"

"It's a simple question. You were in Athens. Why?"

The look Falco gave the older man would have made anyone else take a hurried step back.

"What in hell kind of question is that?"

Cesare shrugged. "A simple one. I asked you—"

"I know what you asked." Falco's eyes narrowed. "Did you have me followed?"

"Nothing so devious." Cesare moved his chair forward

and reached for an elaborately carved wooden box. "Pure Havanas," he said, opening the box to reveal a dozen fat cigars. "They cost the earth. Have one."

"Explain yourself," Falco said sharply, without a glance at the box. "How do you know where I was?"

Another shrug. "I have friends everywhere. Surely you know that by now."

"Then you also know that I was in Athens on business for Orsini Brothers Investments." Falco smiled again, even more coldly. "Perhaps you've heard of us, Father. A privately held company started without any help from you."

Cesare bit the tip off the cigar he'd chosen, turned his head and spat the piece into a wastebasket.

"Even in these bad economic times, we've made our investors wealthy. And we've done it honestly, a concept you couldn't possibly understand."

"You added a private bank to your stable when you were in Athens," Cesare said. "Nicely done."

"Your compliments mean nothing to me."

"But banking was not all you did there," the Don said softly. He looked up; his eyes met Falco's. "My sources tell me that during that same few days, a child—a boy of twelve—held for ransom by insurgents in the northern mountains of Turkey, was somehow miraculously returned to his fam—"

Falco was around the desk in a heartbeat. His hand closed on his father's shirt; he yanked him roughly to his feet.

"What is this?" he snarled.

"Take your hands off me!"

"Not until I get answers. No one followed me. No one. I don't know where you got all this crap but—"

"I was not foolish enough to think anyone could follow you and live to talk about it. Let go of my shirt and perhaps I'll give you an answer."

Falco could feel his heart racing. He knew damned well no one had followed him; he was far too good to let that happen. And, yes, though he would never admit it, there had been more to his trip to Greece than the acquisition of a bank. There were times his old skills came in handy but he kept that part of his life private.

Falco glared at his father. And silently cursed himself for being a fool.

He had not let Cesare get to him in years. Fifteen years, to be exact, on a night one of his father's henchmen had caught him sneaking back into the heavily guarded house at two in the morning.

The Don had been furious, not at where his seventeen-year-old-son might have been, not at how he'd defeated the alarm system, but at how he'd gotten by the silent men who kept watch from the shadows outside the front door and deep within the walled garden.

Falco had refused to explain. He'd done more than that. He'd smirked as only a badass teenage boy could.

Cesare had backhanded him, hard, across the face.

It was the first time his father had hit him, which was, when he'd had time to think about it, a surprise. Not the blow; the surprise was that it had not happened before. There'd always been a hint of violence in the air between father and son; it had grown stronger when Falco reached adolescence.

That night, it had finally erupted.

Falco had stood still under the first blow. The second rocked him back on his heels. The third bloodied his mouth, and when Cesare raised his hand again, Falco grabbed his wrist and twisted the Don's arm high behind his back. Cesare was strong, but at seventeen, Falco was already stronger.

He was also fueled by years of hatred.

"Touch me again," he'd said in a whisper, "and I swear, I'll kill you."

His father's expression had undergone a subtle change. Not fear. Not anger. Something else. Something swift and furtive that should not have been in the eyes of a powerful man who'd just lost a battle, physically as well as figuratively.

Falco's face was badly bruised the next day. His mother questioned it, as did his sisters. He said he'd fallen in the shower. The lie worked but Nicolo, Raffaele and Dante had not been so easy to fool.

"Must have been a pretty awkward tumble," Rafe had said, "to blacken your eye as well as give you a swollen lip."

Yeah, Falco had said calmly, it was.

He never told anyone the truth. Had the beating been too humiliating to talk about? Was it his shock at the intensity of the quicksilver flash of rage that had almost overcome him?

Eventually, he understood.

Power had changed hands that night. It had gone from Cesare to him…and then back to Cesare. What he'd seen in his father's eyes had been the knowledge that despite Falco's vicious threat, he, Cesare, had actually won the battle because Falco had let emotion overtake him. He had lost control of his emotions and somehow, he had no idea how or why, that loss of control gave the other person power.

And now, here he was, fifteen long years later, losing control all over again.

Carefully, he unfisted his hand, let go of Cesare's starched white shirt. Cesare fell back into his chair, his jowly face red with anger.

"If you were not my son…"

"I'm not your son in any way that matters. It takes more than sperm to make a man a father."

A muscle knotted in the Don's jaw. "Are you now a philosopher? Trust me, Falco, in many ways, you are more my son than your brothers."

"What's that supposed to mean?"

"It means that what you so self-righteously claim to hate in me is what is also inside you. The lure of absolute power. The need to control." Cesare's eyes narrowed. "The willingness to shed blood when you know it must be shed."

"Damn you, old man!" Falco leaned over the desk and brought his angry face within inches of the older man's. "I am nothing like you, do you hear? Nothing! If I were, God, if I were…"

He shuddered, drew back, stood straight. What was he doing, letting his father draw him deeper into this quagmire?

"Is this what you wanted to talk about? To tell me you've come up with absolution for yourself by pretending your genes are my destiny? Well, it won't work. I am not you. And this so-called discussion is at an—"

Cesare took something from the folder on his desk and pushed it toward Falco. It appeared to be a glossy page, an advertisement, torn from a magazine.

"Do you know this woman?"

Falco barely spared the picture a glance.

"I know a lot of women," he said coldly. "Surely your spies have told you that."

"Indulge me. Look at her."

What the hell did it matter? Falco picked up the photo. It was an ad for something expensive. Perfume, jewelry, clothing—it was hard to tell.

The focus of the page, though, was clear enough.

It was the woman.

She was seated crossways in an armchair, one long leg on the floor, the other draped over the chair's arm, a shoe with the kind of heel that should have been declared lethal dangling from her toes. She wore lace. Scarlet lace. A teddy. A chemise. He had no idea which it was, only that it showed almost as much cleavage as leg.

A spectacular body. An equally spectacular face. Oval. Delicate. The essence of femininity. High cheekbones, eyes as amber as a cat's, lashes long and thick, the same ebony color as her long, straight hair.

She was smiling at the camera. At the viewer.

At him.

It was, he understood, a deliberate illusion. A damned effective one. Her smile, the tilt of her head, even her posture, dared a man to want her. To be foolish enough to think he could have her. It was a smile that offered as much sexual pleasure as a man could want in a lifetime.

Something hot and dangerous rolled through Falco's belly.

"Well? Do you recognize her?"

He looked up. Cesare's eyes locked on his. Falco tossed the photo on the desk.

"I told you I didn't. Okay? Are we done here?"

"Her name is Elle. Elle Bissette. She was a model. Now she is an actress."

"Good for her."

Cesare took something else from the folder. Another ad? He held it toward Falco, but Falco didn't move.

"What is this? You expect me to spend the next hour playing Name the Celebrity?"

"*Per favore*, Falco. I ask you, please. Look at the photo."

Falco's eyebrows rose. Please? In Italian and in English. He had never heard his father use those words or anything close to them. What the hell, he thought, and reached for the photo.

Bile rose in his throat.

It was the same ad but someone had used a red pen to *X* out her eyes. To trace a crude line of stitches across her lips.

To draw a heavy line across her throat and dab red dots from her throat to her breasts. To circle her breasts in the same bright, vicious crimson.

"Miss Bissette received it in the mail."

"What did the cops say?"

"Nothing. She refuses to contact them."

"She's a fool," Falco said bluntly, "if she won't go to the authorities."

"The parents of the Turkish boy went to you, not the authorities. They feared seeking official help."

"This is America."

"Fear is fear, Falco, no matter where one lives. She is afraid or perhaps she does not trust the police. Whatever the reason, she refuses to contact them." Cesare paused. "Miss Bissette is making a film in Hollywood. The producer is, shall we say, an old friend."

"Ah. I get it now. Your pal's worried about his investment."

"It concerns him, yes. And he needs my help."

"Send him some of your blood money."

"Not my financial help. He needs my help to safeguard Miss Bissette."

"I'm sure your goons will love L.A."

Cesare chuckled. "Can you see my men in Beverly Hills?"

Falco almost laughed. He had to admit, the idea was amusing—and, suddenly, it all came together. The talk of what had happened in Turkey, this conversation about Elle Bissette…

"Okay."

"Okay?"

Falco nodded. "I know some guys who do bodyguard work for celebrities. I'll call around, put you in touch—"

"I am already in touch," Cesare said gently. "With you."

"Me?" This time, Falco did laugh. "I'm an investor, Father, not a bodyguard."

"You did not say that to the people you helped in Turkey."

"That was different. They turned to me and I did what I had to do."

"As I am turning to you, *mio figlio*, and asking that you do what must be done."

Falco's face hardened. "You want some names and phone numbers, fine. Otherwise, I'm out of here."

Cesare didn't answer. Falco snorted, turned on his heel, headed for the door again, changed his mind and decided to exit through the French doors hidden by the heavy drapes. The mood he was in, the last thing he wanted was to risk running in to his mother or his sisters.

"Wait." His father hurried after him. "Take the folder. Everything you need is in it."

Falco grabbed the folder. It was easier than arguing.

By the time he'd taxied to his mid-sixties town house, he'd come up with the names of four men who could do this job and do it well. Once home, he poured a brandy, took the folder and his cell phone and headed outside to his walled garden. It was close to sunset; the air was chill but he liked it out here, with the noise of Manhattan shut away.

There was nothing of much use in the folder. Stuff about the movie; a letter from the producer to Cesare.

And the pictures. The one with her in lace. The marked-up duplicate. And another that his father had not shown him, a photo of Bissette standing on a beach, looking over her shoulder at the camera. No lace. No stiletto heels. She was dressed in a T-shirt and shorts.

Falco put the three pictures on the top of a glass table and looked from one to the other.

The one of her sexy and mysterious was a turn-on if you liked that kind of thing. He didn't. Yeah, he liked crimson and lace and stiletto heels well enough; was there a man who didn't? But the pose was blatantly phony. The smile was false. The woman looking at the camera had no substance. She might have been looking at a million guys instead of him.

The mutilated picture made his gut knot. It was an outright threat, crude but effective.

The third photo was the one that caught him. It was un-selfconscious. Unposed. A simple shot of a beautiful woman walking on a beach, needing no artifice to make her look beautiful.

But there was more to it than that.

She'd sensed someone was watching her. He'd been the watcher often enough in what he thought of as his former life to know how subjects looked when they suspected the unwelcome presence of an observer. He could see it in her eyes. In the angle of her jaw. In the way she held her hair back from her face. Wariness. Fear. Distress.

And more.

Determination. Defiance. An attitude that, despite everything, said, Hey, pal, don't screw with me.

"Goddammit," Falco growled.

Then he grabbed his cell phone and arranged for a chartered plane to fly him to the West Coast first thing in the morning.

CHAPTER TWO

ELLE HAD spent most of the morning in bed with a stranger.

The stranger was tall and good-looking and maybe he was a good kisser. She didn't really know.

The thing was, she didn't like kissing. She knew less about it than, she figured, 98 percent of the female population of the United States over the age of sixteen, but that didn't mean she didn't know how to make kissing seem fantastic, especially with a guy who looked like this.

Kissing, the same as walking and talking, laughing and crying and all the other things an actress did, was part of the job. She had to remember that. This was a movie. Kissing the man in whose arms she lay was, yes, part of the job.

No question that women everywhere would change places with her in a heartbeat. Fans, other actresses... Chad Scott was world-famous. He was box office gold. And, for this scene, at least, he was all hers.

Elle knew how lucky she was. She hated herself for not being able to get into character this morning. Love scenes were always tough but today...

Today, things were not going well at all.

It wasn't her co-star's fault. She'd worried he might be all walking, talking ego, but Chad had turned out to be a nice guy.

He'd shaken her hand when they were introduced days ago, apologized for arriving after everyone else. She knew he hadn't had to do that. They'd spent five minutes in small talk. Then they'd run their lines. Finally, they'd shot their first scene, which was actually a middle scene in the film. Movie scenes were rarely shot sequentially.

Today, they were shooting their first love scene. It was, she knew, pivotal to the story.

The set was simple, just a seemingly haphazard sprawl of blankets spread over the sand near a big Joshua cactus. She was wearing a strapless slip; the camera would only catch her head, her arms and her bare shoulders, suggesting that she was naked. Chad was shirtless and wearing jeans. They were surrounded by a mile of electrical cable, reflectors and boom mikes, and the million and one people it took to film even the simplest scene. Antonio Farinelli, as hot a director as existed, had told the two of them he hoped to do the scene in one take.

So far, there'd been four.

A sudden gust of wind had ruined the first shot but the three others… Her fault, every one. She'd twice blown her lines; the third time she'd looked over Chad's shoulder instead of into his eyes.

Farinelli sounded angrier each time he yelled, "Cut."

Elle sat up, waiting while the director spoke with the lighting guy. Her co-star sat up, too, and stretched. Chad had been really good about all the delays. He'd obviously sensed she was having a problem and he'd made little jokes at his own expense. She knew they were meant to put her at ease. *Heck,* he said, *I'm pretty sure I shaved this morning. And don't feel bad, kid, my wife once told me the ceiling needed paint at a moment just like this.*

Everyone who heard him laughed because he was not just a hot property, he was a hot guy. Elle laughed, too. At least, she did her best to fake it. She was an actress. Illusion was everything.

In real life, she could never have lain in a man's arms and gazed into his eyes as he brought his mouth to hers, but then, reality was a bitch.

And reality was the phone call that had awakened her at three o'clock that morning.

"Darling girl," the low male voice had whispered, "did you get the picture? Did you get my note?" A low, terrible laugh. "You're waiting for me, aren't you, sugar?"

Her heart had slammed into her throat. She'd thrown the telephone on the floor as if it were a scorpion that had crept in under the motel room door. Then she'd run to the bathroom and vomited.

Now, all she could hear was that voice in her head. All she could see was that mutilated ad from the magazine, the note nobody knew about. Bad enough Farinelli knew about the ad. If only he hadn't walked into her on-set trailer just as she'd opened the innocent-looking white envelope she'd found propped against the mirror of her makeup table.

"Elle," Farinelli had said briskly, "about tomorrow's schedule…"

But she wasn't listening. The blood had drained from her head. She'd been as close to fainting as she'd ever been in her life.

"Elle?" Farinelli had said, and he'd plucked the envelope and what she'd taken out of it from her hand.

"Madre di Dio," he'd said, his words harsh with fury. "Where did this come from?"

She had no idea. Once she got her breath back, she told him that. A crazy person must have sent it. She'd had nasty little notes before, especially after the Bon Soir lingerie ads, but this marked-up photo…

Still, anything was possible. Her face was out there. In those two-year-old ads and now in stuff the publicity people for *Dangerous Games* had started planting. It was nothing, she and Farinelli finally agreed, but if she received any more things like this, she was to tell him and they'd go to the police.

Elle had agreed. She'd told herself the photo was a one-shot. Whoever had sent it would surely not contact her again.

Wrong. A few days later, a note arrived in her mail. Its message was horrible. Filthy. Graphic. And it was signed. The signature stunned her but it had to be a hoax. She told herself she would not let it upset her. She was an actress, she could pull it off.

Evidently, she was not as good an actress as she thought.

Farinelli had taken to asking her if she was okay and though she always said yes, certainly, she was fine, she knew he didn't believe it. He'd proved it two days ago when he stopped by her trailer during a break. Was she ill? No, she assured him. Was she upset about her part? No, no, she loved her part. Farinelli had nodded. Then he could only assume that the photo he had seen was still upsetting her because she was most assuredly not herself.

Elle had tried telling him he was wrong. He silenced her with an imperious wave of one chubby hand. He had given the situation much thought. The photo had been *of* her but it had been meant for him. She had been in, what, two, three films? She was almost unknown. He, however, was famous. He was taking a big chance, starring her in *Dangerous Games*. Obviously, someone understood that and wished to ruin his film.

But, by God, he would not permit it. He had millions of his own money tied up in this project and he was not going to let someone destroy him. He was going to contact the police and let them deal with the problem.

Elle couldn't let that happen. The police would poke and pry, ask endless questions, snoop into her past and find that the story of her life that she'd invented had nothing to do with reality.

So she'd resorted to high drama. She pleaded. She wept. She became a *diva*. A risky gambit but she had not come as far as she had by playing things safe. No guts, no glory. Trite and clichéd, maybe, but true. Besides, really, what did she have to lose? A police investigation would destroy the burgeoning career she had worked so hard for. She was twenty-seven, a little long in the tooth to go back to modeling….

More to the point, she could not face her ugly, ugly past all over again.

In the end, Farinelli had thrown up his hands. *"Basta,"* he'd said. "Enough! No police."

A disaster avoided. She'd forced herself to forget the ad, the note, to keep focused on the movie. And then that phone call at three this morning…

"Okay, people" Farinelli said. "Let's try it again."

Elle lay back. Chad leaned over her, waiting for the camera to roll. She felt his breath on her face….

"Hey," her co-star said softly. "You okay?"

"I'm fine," she said, with no conviction at all.

Chad sat up and looked at Farinelli. "Tony? How 'bout we break for lunch?"

The director sighed. "Why not? Okay, people. Lunch. Half an hour."

Chad stood up, held out his hand and helped Elle to her feet. One of Farinelli's gofers rushed over and held out an oversized white terrycloth robe. Elle snuggled into it and Chad squeezed her shoulder.

"Sun's a killer, kid," he said softly. "Some shade, some water and you'll be fine."

Her smile was real this time. He truly was a nice man, a rare species as far as she was concerned.

"Thank you," she said, and she knotted the belt of the robe, slid into the rubber thongs the gofer dropped at her feet and made her way quickly to the half-dozen Airstream trailers clustered like Conestoga wagons awaiting an Indian attack a couple of hundred yards away.

Chad Scott was right, she thought as she went up the two steps to the door of her trailer. Cool air, cool water, some time alone and she'd be fine.

"Absolutely fine," she said as the door swung shut…

A man was standing against the wall just beyond the closed door. Tall. Dark-haired. Wraparound sunglasses. Her brain took quick inventory…and then her heart leaped like a startled cat and she opened her mouth to scream.

But the man was fast. He was on her, turning the locking bolt, one hand over her mouth before the scream erupted. He gripped her by the shoulder with his free hand, spun her around and hauled her back against him.

She could feel every hard inch of his leanly muscled body.

"Screaming isn't going to help," he said sharply.

A waste of time.

Falco could damned near feel the scream struggling to burst from her lips.

To say this wasn't exactly the reception he'd expected was an understatement. He'd spoken with the director, Farinelli, on his cell from the plane. He'd told him when he'd be arriving, more or less, and the director had said that was fine, it gave him lots of time to brief the Bissette woman and that it would be best if he, Falco, met with her in private because she'd probably want his presence on the set kept quiet, so—

"Hey!"

She had kicked him. Useless, as kicks went, because she

was kicking backward and wearing ugly rubber beach thongs, but it told him what he needed to know about whether or not she'd calmed down.

Okay. He'd try again.

"Ms. Bissette. I'm sorry if I startled you but—"

She grunted. Struggled. Her backside dug into his groin. It was a small, rounded backside and under different circumstances, he'd have enjoyed the feel of it—but not when the backside might as well have belonged to a wildcat.

"Dammit," Falco said. He swung her toward him, one hand still clasping her shoulder, the other still clamped over her mouth. "Pay attention, okay? I. Am. Not. Going. To. Hurt. You."

Mistake.

She slugged him. Two quick blows, one to the chest, one to the jaw. He was damned if he knew what to do with her now. He had only two hands and she was already keeping both of them occupied.

"Okay," he said grimly. "You want to play rough? That's fine."

He shoved her, hard. She stumbled back against the door and he went with her, pinned her there with his body. Her hands were trapped against his chest; her legs blocked by his. She was tall but he was a lot taller; her head was tilted back so that she was staring up at him with eyes even more tawny than they'd seemed in the defaced magazine ad.

Eyes filled with terror. And with what he'd seen in the candid photo that had brought him out here.

Defiance.

Okay. Instead of saying to hell with this and walking out the door, he'd try and get through to her one last time.

"Ms. Bissette. My name is Falco Orsini."

Nothing. Still the hot blend of fear and defiance shining in those eyes.

"I'm here to help you."

Fear, defiance and now disbelief.

"Trust me, lady. This isn't my idea of a good time, either. I'm here as a favor. And if you don't calm down and talk to me, I'm gonna walk straight out that door and leave you to handle this thing on your own."

She blinked and he saw confusion sweep across her face. Yeah, but she couldn't be any more confused than he was, unless—unless—

Oh, hell.

"Didn't Farinelli tell you I was coming?"

Another blink. A delicate vertical furrow appeared between her dark eyebrows.

"He said he would. He said you'd want to keep this private and that I should wait for you here, in your trailer."

Her eyes widened. "What?"

It sounded more like "wmf" because his hand was over her lips but there was no mistaking her surprise. Everything was starting to come together. She, a woman who'd been sent a picture defaced by a madman, walks into her trailer and finds a stranger waiting for her….

Merda! That fool, Antonio Farinelli, had never told her he was coming.

"Okay," Falco said, "here's the deal. Somebody sent you a picture." She began to struggle again. He shook his head. "Just listen. You got a picture. A bad one. Your boss wanted to call the cops. You refused. Am I right?"

He could see he was. So far, so good.

"So your boss contacted someone I—someone I know, and that someone contacted me. I agreed to talk to you, check things out, see if there were a way to deal with this so it all goes away quietly. No muss, no fuss. Yes?"

She exhaled sharply. He felt the warmth of her breath flow

over his hand, just as he could feel a fraction of the tension ease from her body. Her eyes were still locked to his, bright and distrustful, but now, at least, curious.

"My name," Falco said, "is Falco Orsini. I, ah, I sometimes do what you might call security consulting. That's why I'm here. I know about the picture, I know that you're worried about it, I know you don't want the authorities involved. I'm here to discuss the situation and offer some advice. That's the only reason I'm here—and the only reason I scared you is because your boss was too stupid to tell you about me." He tried for what he hoped was a reassuring smile. "I'm going to take my hand off your mouth. And maybe we can have that talk. Does that work for you?"

She blinked. Nodded. Now she was wary—but she was ready to listen.

He took his hand from her mouth.

She didn't scream.

Instead, the tip of her tongue came out and slid lightly over her bottom lip. Falco watched its progress. His gaze fell lower, to the rise of her breasts in the vee of her bulky terrycloth robe. He knew what she had under it; he'd watched the scene Farinelli had been filming at a safe distance before he'd slipped into the trailer. What she had on was a slip. Plain. Unadorned. Not like what she'd worn in that ad.

This slip was plain. Sexless.

Not that she was.

She was gorgeous. That hair. Those eyes. That mouth. Still, even with theatrical makeup on, there was another quality to her that he had not seen in the ad. A kind of innocence.

Which was, of course, ridiculous.

She was an actress. She played to the camera. To men. She could be whatever a particular part called for. Maybe she'd decided this part called for wide-eyed and innocent. Not that he gave a damn. He was only interested in her problem, and every problem had a solution.

"Antonio shouldn't have hired you," she said.

"He didn't."

"But you said—"

"I'm doing someone a favor."

"Whatever you're doing, I don't want you here."

Her voice was husky. Shaken.

"Listen," Falco said, "if you want to sit down—"

"I can handle this myself."

"The hell you can," he said bluntly.

Her chin rose. "You don't know what I can and can't do."

"I saw that picture. You can't handle that. No woman can. And there'll be more."

Her gaze sharpened. "What's that supposed to mean?"

Her answer, her body language, gave her away. Falco took off his sunglasses.

"There's been more already," he said grimly. "Hasn't there?"

"No," she said, but far too quickly.

She turned her head away; he reached out, cupped her chin, gave her no choice but to meet his eyes.

"What was it? Another picture? A letter? A phone call?"

No answer, which was answer enough. Her mouth trembled; Falco fought back the illogical desire to take her in his arms and comfort her. It was an uncharacteristic reaction for him in this kind of situation and he didn't like it.

"Have you ever seen a cat play with a mouse?" he said. "He'll keep things going until he tires of the game."

Elle shuddered. "You mean, until he does the things he drew on the picture."

"Yes," he said bluntly.

She nodded. And said, in a low voice, "And you think you can stop him?"

Falco's lips curved in what nobody would ever call a smile. "I know I can."

She stared up at him. "You can keep him from—from doing anything to me?"

"Yes."

"A man of few words," she said, with a little laugh. "How can you be so sure?"

"It's what I do. What I used to do," he said evenly. "I can find him and keep him from hurting you."

Elle stared at this stranger with eyes so dark they resembled obsidian. Why should she believe him? The answer was agonizingly simple.

Because, otherwise, she might not have a life.

Perhaps this man, this Falco Orsini, really could help her.

"If I agreed to let you get involved," she said slowly, "you won't—you won't contact the police?"

"No."

"Because, uh, because the publicity," she said, scrambling for a reason he'd accept, "because the publicity—"

"I told you. I'll handle this alone. No cops."

"What would you do, if I hired you?"

"You can't hire me. Remember what I said? I'm here as a favor. As for what I'll do… Leave that to me."

"The thing is…I wouldn't want anyone to know I had a-a bodyguard. There'd be talk. And questions. And questions are the last thing I want."

"I already figured that."

"So, how would we do this, then? I mean, how could you watch over me, go after whoever this is, do whatever you need to do without people knowing?"

Falco had considered that dilemma during the six-hour

flight from New York. There were lots of ways to move into someone's life to provide protection and search out information without raising questions. The idea was to assume a role other people would accept. He could pass himself off as her driver. Her assistant. Her personal trainer.

Personal trainer was pretty much what he'd decided on. Hollywood was filled with actors and actresses who worked on their bodies 24/7. He was fit; he'd look the part. And it would give him access to her no matter where she went.

Okay. Personal trainer it would be...

"Mr. Orsini?"

"Falco," he said, looking down into her eyes. He saw the rise and fall of her breasts, remembered the soft, lush feel of her against him, and he knew he wasn't going to pretend to be her trainer after all.

"Simple," he said calmly. "We'll make people think I'm your lover."

She stared at him. Then she gave a little laugh.

"That's crazy," she said. "No one will believe—"

"Yeah," he said, his voice low and rough, "yeah, they will. Falco reached out, gathered Elle in his arms and kissed her.

CHAPTER THREE

THE FEEL of her mouth under his was incredible.

Warm. Silken. And soft. Wonderfully soft.

Not that he cared about that.

He was kissing her only to wipe that smug little smile from her face. To show her, in no uncertain terms, that they sure as hell could play the part of lovers, fool anybody who saw them.

Did she think she was the only one who could stick to a script?

Or did she think a bodyguard was too far out of her class to seem a convincing lover for a woman like her?

She was fighting him. Trying to twist free of his arms, to drag her lips from his. To hell with that. That who-do-you-think-you-are attitude of hers deserved a blunt response. She was wrong and he wasn't going to let her go until she knew it.

"No," she gasped against his mouth, but she might as well have saved her breath. Falco speared his fingers into her hair, tilted her face to his and kept on kissing her.

So what if she tasted of honey and cream? If she felt warm and soft against him? Those things were meaningless. This was about nothing else than teaching her that she couldn't laugh at Falco Orsini and get away with it.

He nipped lightly at her bottom lip. Touched the tip of his tongue to the seam of her mouth. With heart-stopping suddenness, she stopped fighting, stopped struggling.

She leaned into him, sighed and parted her lips. His tongue plunged deep.

The taste of her made his mind blur.

And his body react.

In an instant, he came fully erect, not just aroused but hard as stone, so hard it was painful. Desire pulsed hot and urgent in his blood. He slid his hands to her shoulders, cupped them, lifted her to her toes, drew her so close he could feel the race of her heart against his.

This was what he had wanted since he'd seen her in that first, unaltered ad. The eyes and mouth that promised passion, the made-for-sex body—

The knife that pressed against his belly caught him fully unaware.

Falco went absolutely still.

Where she'd gotten the knife was irrelevant. The feel of it wasn't. With instincts and sharp reflexes honed by his time in Special Forces, he locked one hand around her forearm and grabbed her wrist with the other, bending it back until the knife clattered to the floor. He kicked it into a corner, saw that it wasn't a knife at all but the slim plastic handle of a hairbrush. Not that it mattered.

It was the intent that counted.

"Let go of me!"

Her hands clawed for his face. He grunted, shoved her back against the unyielding door, used his weight to keep her in place. The only way she could hurt him was if she managed to throw him off and that was about as likely as the trailer sprouting wings. He had at least seven inches in height on her and probably eighty, ninety pounds of muscle.

"Stop it," he snarled.

That only made her fight harder. Falco tightened his grasp on her wrists, brought her hands to her sides and pinned them to the door.

"I said, stop it! You want me to hurt you, I will."

She made a choked sound but it wasn't of rage, it was of terror. Her face, bright with color a moment ago, blanched. Those enormous topaz eyes turned glassy.

He'd flown out here to protect this woman. Instead, he was scaring her half to death. Kissing her had been a straight and simple matter of ego and he wasn't into BS like that. He was who he was; he didn't need anybody's applause to do whatever job he set out to do, certainly not a client's. He'd let his pride, whatever you wanted to call it, get in the way.

And he didn't like it, not one bit.

"Listen to me."

She wouldn't. She was lost in her own world, fearing the worst.

"Ms. Bissette," he said sharply. "Elle. Pay attention. I'm not going to hurt you."

Her eyes met his.

Hell. He'd seen a dog look at him like this once, years back when he was just a kid. He'd found the animal wandering an alley not far from the Orsini mansion in Greenwich Village. Its ribs had showed; there were marks he hadn't wanted to identify on its back. *Come on, boy*, he'd said, holding out his hand, but the creature had looked at him through eyes that said it damned well knew his soft voice didn't mean a thing.

He'd won the dog's trust by squatting down, holding out his arms, showing his hands were empty. What was the human equivalent of that kind of message?

Falco cleared his throat.

"Okay. Here's what happens next. I'll let go of you and step back. You stay where you are. No hands, no fists, no weapons. And we'll talk. That's it. We'll just talk."

He gave it a couple of seconds. Then he did what he'd told her he'd do. Another couple of seconds went by. She didn't move. Neither did he. That was some kind of success, wasn't it? A little color had returned to her face. Another plus. Finally, she took a deep breath.

"I want you to leave."

Her voice was low but steady. Her eyes had lost that terrified glitter. Good. Maybe now they really could talk.

"Look, Ms. Bissette—"

"I said—"

"I heard you. But we need to discuss this."

"We have nothing to discuss."

She was back. He could see it in the way she held herself, in the lift of her chin, the steadiness of her gaze.

"Actually, we do. I'm sorry if I frightened you but—"

"Frightened me?" Her eyes narrowed. "You disgusted me!"

"Excuse me?"

"Putting your hands on me. Your mouth on me." Her chin went up another notch. "Men like you are…you're despicable!"

Falco felt a muscle jump in his cheek. He'd been called similar names, a long time back, though they'd been names that were far more basic. It happened when you were a kid and your old man was Cesare Orsini.

He'd learned to respond to such remarks with his fists.

Not this time, obviously. This time, he flashed a cold smile.

"Trust me, Ms. Bissette. The feeling is mutual. I'm not into women who look into a camera as if they want to screw the guy behind it. I was simply making a point."

"You made it. You're contemptible."

Falco gave an exaggerated sigh. "Disgusting, despicable, contemptible. Yeah, yeah, yeah. I've heard it all before."

Elle Bissette folded her arms. "I'll bet you have."

"You said we couldn't fool anybody if we pretended we were lovers. I figured I could save us ten minutes of talk by showing you that you were wrong."

"Well, you didn't. And I wasn't. I'm an actress but playing at being your lover would take more talent that even I possess."

Her insults almost made him laugh. From poor little victim to haughty aristocrat in the blink of an eye. Damned right, she was an actress.

But he was willing to bet that her terror a little while ago had not been an act.

"Look," he said in as conciliatory a tone as he could manage, "why don't we start over? We'll go somewhere, have a cup of coffee, you'll fill me in on why you need a bodyguard—"

"I do not need a bodyguard. Are you deaf? I want you out of here, right now."

She pointed an elegant hand at the door and tossed her head. Her hair, a mane of jet black, flew around her face. He'd bet she'd practiced the gesture in front of a mirror until it looked just right.

"Get out or I'll scream so loud it'll bring half the world running."

Enough, Falco thought grimly. He took a step forward and clasped her elbows.

"That's fine," he said coldly. "Go right ahead. Scream your head off."

"You think I won't? I will! And five minutes after that, you'll be in jail."

"You left out a step. The part where the cops show up." He tightened his hold on her and hauled her to her toes, his head lowered so their faces were inches apart. "They'll want to have a nice, long chat with you, baby. Are you up for that?"

She stared at him. The color drained from her face and she became still.

"What's the matter, Ms. Bissette? Don't you like that idea?" She didn't answer and he flashed a smile as cold as a New York winter. "Maybe, if we're really lucky, the paparazzi will come by along with the cops. Then you can talk to the whole world."

Whatever fight was left in her was gone. She went limp under his hands, her head drooped forward and all at once he thought, to hell with this! He had not flown 3,000 miles to play games. She found him disgusting? Her prerogative. She had a reason to keep the cops away? Her prerogative again. She was not his problem, none of this was. How he'd let himself be drawn into the mess was beyond him but no way was he going to get drawn in any deeper.

The lady had said "no," and "no" it was.

"Relax," he said, his tone flat as he let go of her and stepped back. "You don't need to scream to get rid of me. Just move away from the door and I'm out of here."

She didn't move. He rolled his eyes, shouldered past her and reached for the knob.

"Wait a minute."

Falco looked over his shoulder. Elle Bissette swallowed; he saw the muscles move in her throat. Which color were here eyes? Amber or topaz? The thought was so completely inappropriate, it made him angry.

"What now?" he growled.

"Mr. Orsini." She hesitated. "This is your—your line of work? You're a bodyguard?"

He smiled thinly. "I am any number of things, Ms. Bissette, but it's a little late to ask for my CV."

"The thing is…I didn't ask for a bodyguard."

"Here's a news flash, baby. I didn't ask for the job."

"But you said someone sent you."

"I said someone I know told me you had a problem and asked me to check it out." His mouth twisted. "And here I am."

"Look, it's not my fault you agreed to do a favor for a friend and—"

"He isn't a friend and I don't do favors for anybody." Falco heaved out a breath. Why get into any of that? How he'd come to be here didn't matter, especially since he was about to leave. "It's a long story and it doesn't change the facts. I came here because I was under the impression you needed help." Another thin smile. "I was wrong."

"You *were* wrong," she said quickly. "You can see for yourself, I'm just fine."

He thought of the terror that had shone in her eyes a little while ago. Well, maybe it was true. Maybe she was fine. Maybe all that fear had been strictly of him.

"Really, I'm fine. I'm just wondering why you…why someone would have thought otherwise."

Falco dug his hands into the pockets of his flannel trousers. "You posed for a magazine ad," he said. "A provocative one."

Her chin rose again. He'd seen pro boxers with the same habit. It wasn't a good one, not if you didn't want to end up in trouble.

"It was a lingerie ad, Mr. Orsini, not an ad for—for Hershey's chocolate."

He grinned. "No argument there, Ms. Bissette." His grin faded. "Fifty thousand lovesick idiots went out and bought their girlfriends whatever it is you were wearing in that ad, then wondered why it didn't look on them the way it looked on you."

She stiffened. He could almost see the gears working. She

was trying to figure out if what he'd said was a compliment or an insult.

"For your information," she said coldly, "statistics show that women are the target audience for lingerie ads."

"Great. So fifty thousand broads went out and bought that outfit, put it on, looked in the mirror and wondered what the hell had gone wrong."

For a fraction of a second, she looked as if she wanted to laugh. Then that chin rose again.

"Is there a point to this, Mr. Orsini?"

"Damned right. All those people looked at an ad and saw an ad." His voice became chill. "One sicko saw something else and decided to—what's today's favorite psychobabble term? He decided to 'share' what he saw with you."

A flush rose in her cheeks. "You've seen what that—that person sent me."

Falco nodded. "Yes."

He expected a rant. Indignation, that Farinelli had sent the thing to someone. Instead, she shuddered.

"It was—it was horrible," she whispered.

A fraction of his anger dissipated. She looked tired and vulnerable; she was frightened even though she was determined to claim she wasn't, but she wasn't going to do anything to protect herself. It made no sense.

"It was worse than horrible." He waited a beat. "Why won't you go to the cops?"

"You said it yourself. It was just the work of some— some crazy."

"Crazies can be dangerous," Falco said. "He should be found."

She stared at him, her eyes suddenly filled with that same despair he'd seen in the photo of her on the beach.

"That would mean publicity."

"Publicity's better than turning up dead."

His blunt statement was deliberate. He'd hoped to shock her into telling him the real reason she didn't want to go to the police—he'd have bet a thousand bucks there wasn't an actor or actress on the planet who didn't want publicity, good or bad—but he could see that wasn't going to happen.

"It's just a prank," she said, very calmly. "Stuff like that happens. I mean, this is Hollywood."

"Has he contacted you again?"

"You already asked me that. I told you, he hasn't."

She'd lied again. So what? So what if there was more to this than she was letting on? Fifteen minutes from now, he'd be on a plane heading back to New York.

"Just that one thing?" he heard himself ask. "Nothing else?"

"Isn't that what I just said?" A smile as false as the one she wore in that lingerie ad curved her lips. "Look, I'm not worried. Really. There's security on the set. I have an alarm system in my house." Another smile. A toss of the head. Forget despair. What he saw in those topaz eyes now was dismissal. "At any rate, thank you for coming to see me."

Falco shrugged. "No problem."

She held out her hand. It was a queen's gesture. She was discharging him, her subject.

Something flickered inside him.

Had that softening of her mouth under his, that barely perceptible sigh, really all been an act? Had she been diverting him so he wouldn't expect that phony knife at his belly? Or had it been real? That sudden, sexy little sound she'd made. The way she'd parted her lips beneath his.

One step forward. One tug on those slender fingers extended toward him. Then she'd be in his arms, her breasts soft against his hard chest, her thighs against his, her lips his for the taking. And he would take them, he'd kiss her again and again, taking each kiss deeper than the last until she moaned and rose to him, whispered her need and her hunger against his mouth...

Dammit, was he insane?

She didn't go for men like him. Hey, that was fine. He didn't go for women like her. And he sure as hell wasn't turned on by women who flaunted their sexuality, who all but invited a faceless sea of men to get off on thinking what it would be like to take her to bed.

Falco ignored her outstretched hand.

"Goodbye, Ms. Bissette," he said, and he opened the door of the trailer and stepped briskly into the heat of the desert.

The afternoon's shoot began badly and went downhill from there.

It made the morning's attempts look good.

Everybody was unhappy.

The heat was awful; they'd been breaking early because of it but Farinelli announced that they were going to get this scene filmed or, *per Dio*, nobody was leaving!

Elle just could not get the scene right. Not her fault, she kept telling herself. The encounter with Falco Orsini had shaken her. She'd done her best to be polite to him at the end but it hadn't been easy. Finding him in her trailer, a stranger so tall, so powerful that he'd seemed to fill the space...

And the way he'd kissed her, as if he could make her want to kiss him back.

Some women might; even she knew that. Not her, though. She hated the whole sex thing. It was like a bad joke, a woman hired for her sex appeal in an ad, but it wasn't a joke, it was the terrible truth. A man's wet mouth, his rough hands...

Falco Orsini's mouth had not been wet. It had been warm

and hard and possessive but not wet. And his hands…hard, yes. Strong. But he hadn't touched her roughly….

Elle gave herself a mental shake.

So what? The point was, he'd had no right to kiss her even though he'd done it in response to her telling him she and he could never pretend they were lovers. Besides, it didn't matter. He would not be her bodyguard. Nobody would. Nobody would poke and pry and ask questions she had no intention of answering….

"…listening to me, Elle?"

She blinked. Antonio was standing close to her while everyone waited. "This is a love scene. A very important one. You must convey passion. Desire. Hunger. And you must do it with your eyes, your hands, your face. There is no kissing in this scene, *sì*? There is only teasing. Of your character, of Chad's character, of the audience." He took her arm, looked up at her, his expression determined. "You can do this. Relax. Forget the cameras, the crew. Forget everything but whatever brought that look to your face in the advertisement you did for Bon Soir."

Elle almost laughed. She'd had small movie roles before but that ad had gotten her this big part. What if people knew that "that look" had been the lucky result of an unlucky sinus infection? A heady combination of aspirin, decongestant and nasal-and-throat spray had miraculously translated to glittering eyes, slumberous lids and parted lips.

Better not to mention that, of course.

"One last try," Farinelli said softly. "I want you to imagine yourself in the arms of a man whose passion overcomes your most basic inhibitions, a man who stirs you as no other ever could. Imagine a flesh-and-blood lover, *bella*, one you have known and never forgotten. Put Chad out of your mind."

Chad rolled his eyes. "Damn, Antonio. You really know how to hurt a guy."

The joke was deliberate. A tension reliever, and it worked. Everybody laughed. Elle managed a smile. Farinelli patted her hand, stepped away, then raised his hand like the Pope about to give a benediction.

"And, action!"

Elle lay back in her co-star's arms. Her heart was racing with nerves. What had she been thinking, letting her agent convince her to take this part? What Antonio wanted of her was impossible. She couldn't do it, couldn't look into a man's eyes and want him not even when it was make-believe.

Having a man's hands on her. His wet mouth on her mouth. God, oh, God…

"Look at me," Chad's character said. It was a line of dialogue he'd repeated endless times today. Elle looked up, just as *she* had done endless times today….

And saw not his movie-star handsome face, but the beautiful, proud, masculine face of Falco Orsini.

Obsidian eyes. Thin, aristocratic nose. Chiseled jaw and a hard, firm mouth—a mouth that she could still remember for its warmth, its hunger, its possessiveness.

An ache swept through her body, heat burned from her breasts to low in her belly…

"And, cut!"

Elle blinked. She stared at the man looking down at her. Chad, her co-star, who flashed a toothy grin.

"Elle, *mia bella*!" Antonio Farinelli hurried toward her. She heard a smattering of applause, a couple of whistles as he held out his hands and helped her to her feet. "*Brava*, Elle. That was *perfetto*!" He brought his fingers to his lips and kissed them. "The screen will sizzle!"

Chad rose beside her and winked. "I don't know who you were thinkin' about, honey, but he is sure one lucky guy."

* * *

A quarter of a mile away, half-concealed by a Joshua tree, Falco Orsini slammed a pair of high-powered binoculars into a leather case and tossed it into the front seat of his rented SUV.

What a hell of a performance! Elle Bissette and a cameraman. Elle Bissette and an actor. And when this movie hit the theaters, Elle Bissette and a couple of million faceless men.

She was hot for every guy in the world.

Except him.

No that he gave a damn.

What got to him was that he'd flown 3,000 miles and she'd sent him packing. Her choice, but he couldn't stop thinking about that look in her eyes in the beach photo and again in the trailer, a look that spelled FEAR in capital letters.

Something was happening and no way was he leaving until he knew what it was. Falco got into the SUV and settled in to wait.

CHAPTER FOUR

AN HOUR passed before he saw her. She was heading for the cars parked near the set. He'd figured her for something bright and expensive. He was right about the bright part, but expensive? He smiled. The lady drove a red Beetle.

He'd been wrong about her destination, too. He'd figured her for a rented house in Palm Springs or maybe a glitzy hotel but she headed northwest. To L.A.? It was a fairly long drive but this was Friday. She was probably heading home for the weekend.

Following her wasn't a problem. There was plenty of traffic, plus she turned out to be a conservative driver, staying in the right-hand lane and doing a steady 65 miles per hour.

He settled in a few of cars behind her.

After a while, her right turn signal light blinked on. She took an exit ramp that led to the kind of interchange he was pretty sure existed only in California, a swirl of interlocking roads that looked as if somebody had dumped a pot of pasta and called the resultant mess a highway system.

Freeway. That was what they called them here. He remembered that when the Bissette woman took a freeway headed north.

Still no problem but where was she going?

Another thirty minutes went by before her turn signal

came on again. This time, the exit led into a town so small he'd have missed it had he blinked. Following her wasn't so simple now, especially after she hung a couple of lefts and ended up on a two-lane country blacktop.

Traffic was sparse. A couple of cars, a truck carrying a load of vegetables, that was about all.

Dusk had fallen. There was no other traffic now. Bissette's taillights came on. Falco kept his lights off and hung farther back.

They'd been on the road a long time and the passing minutes had only made his suspicions sharpen. Why was she so determined to handle the mess she was in all by herself?

Why was she so smugly certain nobody would buy into him as her lover?

Did she want him to believe she could convince a million horny guys looking at her in an ad or in a movie that they turned her on, but that she couldn't play the same act one on one with him?

His hands tightened on the steering wheel.

Was that the real reason he was tailing her? To confront her again, show her what could happen if he wanted it to happen, if he kissed her not to make a point but to make her damned well admit she wanted to respond to him, that it wouldn't take any acting at all for her to come alive in his arms?

"Merda!"

Falco slowed the SUV to a crawl. Was he going nuts?

It was years, hell, it was more than a decade since he'd cared about proving himself to anybody. And it had never, ever involved a woman. "The Orsini Stud," his brothers had laughingly called him when they had been in their teens. They'd all done just fine in that department but yeah, some of the local girls had burned extra hot for the neighborhood bad boy.

It had been like that as he got older, too; it still was.

Women, beautiful women, were easy to come by. Women even more beautiful than Elle Bissette. Women who didn't play games. So, what was he doing following her into the middle of nowhere?

It wasn't logical, and it wasn't like him.

Okay. It had been a long day. He needed to kick back, have a drink, a meal…

Yes, but what was Bissette doing in the middle of nowhere? Maybe that was the real question. This all but empty road, curving now like a snake as it climbed into the mountains, tall trees on either side. It wasn't a good place to be if some crazy was after you. Crowds. Bright lights. People. There was safety in numbers. A cliché but also a fact.

Falco frowned.

Maybe the whole thing was a lie.

Maybe it was her idea of publicity. Or the director's. He didn't think so, after talking with Farinelli, after seeing that mutilated ad, but anything was possible.

Or maybe she was all the way out here to meet some guy. A lover. A woman like this, lush and sensual, sure as hell would have a man around. A weekend of sex, of lying in her lover's arms, of giving him what she had made clear she would never give Falco, her body naked under his, her hands on him, her mouth…

His body reacted so quickly, so completely, that it was embarrassing.

Forget needing a drink. What he needed was a run, a long one. Or a workout. Better still, he needed both. He'd been in L.A. before, he knew a couple of gyms where he could sweat whatever this was out of his system and—

Falco blinked. Bissette's taillights, two dots of crimson bleeding far into the distance, flashed brightly, then disappeared.

Had she made him?

He picked up speed. Slowed when he reached the approximate location where she'd seemingly vanished. Without headlights, it was difficult to see much of anything, but, yeah, he spotted something, a pair of old wooden posts to the left of the road and between them, a rutted track barely wide enough for a car. The VW had taken it; he could see its taillights and, in the sweep of its headlights, the murky outline of a house in a small clearing.

The lady had reached her destination.

A muscle flickered in Falco's jaw.

A strange place for an actress to rendezvous with her lover. A dangerous place, if she wasn't meeting anyone and would be here alone, but hey, not his problem…

"Dammit," Falco said. He pulled to a cleared space fifty feet ahead, parked and got out of the SUV.

Elle sighed with relief as her headlights picked up the shape of the cabin.

She parked her VW under a soaring pine, stepped out and shut the door after her. The clearing was dark; there were stars overhead but the moon had not yet risen.

No matter. She knew every foot of the clearing and the cabin by heart.

And loved all of it.

She'd rented it for a while and she'd been heartbroken when the owner decided to sell it or tear it down. She couldn't blame him. The cabin was small, it needed lots of work, and the ski resort that had once been planned a few miles away had never materialized.

Nobody wanted the run-down cabin but her. It was her sanctuary but she couldn't afford to buy it.

And then, a miracle. She'd signed with Bon Soir. Her contract called for more money than she'd ever imagined she might earn and she'd taken the entire check and plunked it down on the cabin.

Now, it was hers.

She was still fixing it up. It needed a new porch, a new roof, but what did that matter? It belonged to her. Nobody else. No one knew about it, either. It was the one place where she could relax, be herself...

Be safe.

She'd always felt safe here, despite the isolation. The cabin, the surrounding woods, took her back to her childhood. Part of her childhood, she thought quickly, the only part she ever wanted to remember, when her mother was still alive and there'd been just the two of them living in a cabin like this in a woods like this...

An owl called from the trees.

Elle jumped. Silly. The woods were home to lots of creatures, none of them frightening. It was the day that had left her feeling unsettled, she thought as she climbed the porch steps. The scene that just wouldn't end, the movie role she should never have taken...

The man.

Falco Orsini.

Elle took her keys from her pocket and unlocked the door.

How dare he show up the way he had? Without warning, without permission.

She stepped inside the cabin, shut the door behind her.

Part of it was Farinelli's fault. The director had no right going behind her back; he should have told her he was going to hire a bodyguard and she'd have told him to do no such thing. But that man. Orsini. Entering her trailer. Waiting for her there. Acting as if he owned her. Kissing her. Forcing her into his arms, forcing her to endure the feel of his hands, his body, his mouth.

A tremor went through her.

Awful, all of it…

It *had* been awful… Hadn't it?

She could still feel his embrace. The strength of his arms. The hardness of his body. The warmth of his mouth. And— and the sudden, incredible quickening of her blood.

No. That was impossible. What she'd felt had been disgust. What else would a woman feel when a man touched her? She knew all she needed to know about men and their needs, their appetites, their hunger. Some women endured it all, some pretended to like those things. Not her. She knew. She had always known, and what did that matter?

Falco Orsini had burst into her life and now he was gone.

All that talk about protecting her… Elle tossed her purse aside. Baloney, her mama would have said. He had his own agenda; hadn't he proved it by trying to kiss her? Men always had their own agendas. Her co-star acted like Mr. Nice Guy, but, really, it was only because he wanted to get this movie over with. Her director wanted the same thing and had proved he'd do anything to have it happen, including hiring a bodyguard that he had to know she would not want.

Especially a bodyguard like Falco Orsini.

The hard, handsome face. The powerful body. The low, husky voice. The veneer of good manners laid over the persona of a street tough.

Elle shook her head, reminded herself she'd come all the way up here so she could spend the weekend ridding herself of all those thoughts and reached for the nearest light switch.

Nothing.

Click. Click. Click.

Dammit, the light wasn't coming on. Moving carefully, feeling her way, trying to ignore the sudden unease tiptoeing up her spine, she made her way to a table and reached for the lamp centered on it.

Click. Click. Click.

The hair rose on the nape of her neck. Two bulbs dying at the same time? Coincidence? Yes. It had to be. Hadn't she just thought about the fact that nobody even knew the cabin existed? She'd kept it as her secret hideaway from the start. She had an apartment in Studio City, but this was where she came to restore her soul. Mama would have said that, too. The woods were like a cathedral where you went to find peace.

Coincidence, absolutely.

Briskly, she moved forward, hand outstretched, feeling for the little round table beside the sofa. Yes. There it was. Her fingers found the slender column of the lamp centered on it, skated up its cool surface, closed around the switch.

The light came on.

Elle breathed a sigh of relief…

And saw what had been hung on the planked pine wall beside the fireplace.

A scream rose in her throat but she couldn't get it out. It seemed to take forever before it burst, full-blown, into the dark silence of the night.

Falco was standing on the edge of the woods that surrounded the cabin, asking himself—for the third time—just what, exactly, he was doing here.

He'd come out of curiosity or maybe out of anger and a slightly dented ego, and none of that justified following her here. Elle Bissette didn't want his help. She didn't want any part of him. Fine. End of story. By now, he should have been on a plane, halfway to New York.

His mouth thinned. Hell, he thought, and he turned and started jogging toward the road.

He'd already made a fool of himself, trying to protect this woman. Why would he do it again? She wanted to spend the night in a place that looked like a leftover from a *Friday the 13th* movie? Her business, not—

Her scream tore apart the night.

Falco turned and ran to the house. He charged up the porch steps. This was not the textbook response to trouble. He had no weapon, no knowledge of what awaited him, but that scream…

The door opened and Elle flew through it, straight into his outstretched arms.

"No," she shrieked, "no, no, no…"

"Ms. Bissette. Elle. It's me. Falco Orsini."

He knew she couldn't hear him, not in the state she was in, eyes wide with terror, face white with it. Panting, sobbing, she beat at him with her fists but he had no time to worry about that. Instead, he shoved her behind him, braced himself to take on whoever was in there…

Nobody.

The cabin, brightly illuminated by a lamp at the far end, was empty.

Falco turned to Elle, huddled in the corner of the porch. Her breath was coming in desperate little gasps. Her teeth were chattering. She was cold and shaking and he cursed, reached for her and gathered her into his arms.

"Elle. You're safe. You're with me."

Slowly, she raised her head and focused on his face. "Mister—Mister Orsini?"

"Yes. That's right. Tell me what happened. Was someone waiting for you here?"

She shook her head. "N-no."

"But something scared you. What was it?"

"I saw—I saw…" Her expression changed, her voice was still weak but not it was tinged with suspicion. "What—what are you doing here?"

"I followed you."

"You followed…?" Her hands flattened against his chest. She pushed back a couple of inches. "Why?"

Why, indeed? "We can talk about that later. Right now you need to tell me what frightened you."

Her eyes clouded; she dragged them from his and looked down. "It's—it's nothing. A—a spider."

Falco's mouth twisted. "That's bull and you know it." He cupped her face, forced her to meet his steady gaze. "Here's the bottom line, lady. You won't call the cops? I will."

"No. You have no right—"

"You need help. If not from me, then from the police."

"All right!" She took a breath. "Someone—someone left something here. Something for me."

He felt his belly knot. "Another picture?"

She shook her head. Her hair whispered across his hands like ebony silk. "Not a picture. An—an animal. A dead animal."

Falco nodded. "Okay. Here's what you're going to do. My SUV is parked on the road about fifty feet up. Here are the keys. Go to it, get inside, lock the doors and—"

"No!" Her fingers curled into his jacket. "I don't want to be alone."

Falco put his arms around her again. She stiffened but she let him hold her. He could feel her heart racing. She felt fragile and female and hell, any man would show a woman compassion at a moment like this.

"All right. Forget the SUV. You stay here while I check things out."

"Okay."

Her voice was low and shaky. He'd have liked it better if she'd given him a hard time. She was tough, he already knew that, and this show of obedience told him, even more than her pallor and her trembling, that she was far too close to shock.

"Good girl." Her eyes had not left his. Instinct took over. He bent his head and brushed his lips gently over hers, told himself it was simply another way of offering her the reassurance she needed. Her mouth trembled at the touch of his; the warmth of her breath was a shocking contrast to the icy feel of her skin. "I'll be right back."

She nodded. He stroked a strand of hair back from her cheek. Then he took a deep breath and stepped inside the cabin.

It wasn't much. Anybody expecting the palatial digs of a movie star would have been disappointed. One room, simply furnished. A couple of small tables. A couple of chairs. A door to his left stood open and led into a no-nonsense bathroom. Sink, shower, toilet. An alcove to the right held an apartment-sized stove, refrigerator and sink.

The lamp at the far end of the cabin burned as brightly as the sun.

There was a light switch by the door. A lamp on a table a couple of feet away. Why would Elle have ignored both, made her way through a dark cabin to reach the most distant light source in the room?

He tried the wall switch. The table lamp. Got useless clicks both times. Coincidence? He doubted it. A quick look confirmed it. There was no bulb in the wall fixture, none in the lamp.

Someone had set things up so Elle would be drawn farther into the room.

To the wall beside the fireplace.

To something he could see hanging on that wall.

Falco moved forward slowly. The thing on the wall became easier to identify. His belly knotted. Yes, it was an animal. A possum? A squirrel?

A cat. Yes, but not a real—

"Falco?"

He spun around. Elle stood in the doorway, hands clasped at her waist, face a pale oval against the darkness behind her. Her gaze was fixed on the wall.

"Is it—is it dead?"

"It's okay," he said, but she shook her head. Falco moved toward her. "Honestly, baby, it's okay. It isn't a real animal, it's a toy. A toy cat."

Elle made a little sound. She began to sway. Falco cursed and got to her just before she went down in a boneless heap.

CHAPTER FIVE

IT COULD have been an act.

Bissette was an actress, wasn't she? Maybe she thought she could play him for sympathy if she did an old-time swoon.

But the light-as-air feel of her limp body in his arms, the way her head lolled back against his shoulder, was all too real. She was out like the proverbial light.

Falco cursed under his breath and carried her to the futon. "Elle," he said urgently. "Elle, can you hear me?"

Nothing. Her face was devoid of color. For all he knew, she was going into shock.

The cabin was cold. And damp. There was wood and kindling on the fireplace hearth but no way was he going to let her remain here long enough for a blazing fire to matter. The time for her to make her own decisions was over.

When he left this place, so would she.

A patchwork quilt, almost translucent with age, was neatly folded across a ladder-back maple chair. He shook open the quilt, drew it over her then lay his fingers against her throat.

Good.

Her pulse, though rapid, was strong and steady. She'd stopped shaking and now tinges of color were starting to stain her cheeks.

His throat tightened.

God, she was beautiful. Even now, with no makeup, her hair wild, she was the most beautiful woman he'd ever seen.

And what did that matter at a time like this?

He had to get Elle Bissette up and moving and out of this dreary, isolated place. She might not want a bodyguard but she was in no condition to make that determination. She was his responsibility. For the moment, anyway.

A man didn't turn his back on his duty.

Falco went quickly to the alcove that passed for a kitchen, pulled a dish towel from a rack, checked the minuscule fridge, found a bottle of water. Halfway to the futon he made a quick detour, ripped the toy cat from the wall and put it aside.

Elle gave a soft moan.

He squatted next to her, opened the bottle of water, poured some onto the towel and patted it over her forehead and cheeks.

"Elle," he said firmly. "Open your eyes."

A sigh. A murmur. A flutter of lashes so long they seemed to curve against her cheekbones. Her eyes opened. Confusion glittered in their amber depths. Then she gave a hoarse cry, jerked upright and went for his face.

"Dammit," he said, and caught her wrists. "Elle. Take it easy. You're all right. It's me. Falco."

She stilled. Her eyes cleared. "Falco?" she whispered.

He let out a breath he didn't know he'd been holding.

"Yeah," he said gruffly. "It's me."

She fell back against the futon. "What—what happened?"

"You fainted."

"That's impossible. I've never fainted in my life."

Her voice was thready but the determination was there just the same. He would have laughed if he hadn't figured that would only send her into attack mode again and there wasn't time for that.

"Yeah," he said, "well, there's a first time for everything." He leaned forward, wrapped a strong arm around her shoulders, drew her toward him and held out the water bottle. "Drink."

"What is that?"

Falco rolled his eyes. "Gin and tonic with a slice of lime. It's water, babe. H_2O."

"But I'm not—"

"Thirsty. Do you ever do anything without an argument?"

She gave him the glare he figured the Medusa had used to turn men to stone. That was good, considering she'd been out cold only a few minutes ago. Then she snatched the bottle from his hand, put her head back and took a long drink. He watched the play of muscle in her throat, watched a trickle of water make its way over her bottom lip.

All he had to do was lean in, put the tip of his tongue to that tiny bit of moisture…

Falco shot to his feet. "Okay," he said brusquely. "Are you ready to tell me what just happened?"

"What do you mean, what just happened? I passed out."

"Somebody that knows about this place broke in to it and left something for you."

"Oh, God." Her voice turned thready. "The cat."

Idiot, he said to himself, and squatted beside her again.

"It was a toy, Elle. It wasn't real."

"I know. You said so."

He nodded. "But you fainted anyway."

Her gaze met his, then skittered away. "From relief."

"Or because that toy has some meaning to you."

"No," she said quickly. Much too quickly.

"I saw you, Elle. You thought the cat was real… That was bad." A muscle knotted in his jaw. "But finding out it was a toy was even worse." His eyes drilled into hers. "Why?"

Elle gave him another of those cold glares. He could see

the defiance, the tough independence coming back, but he knew enough this time to recognize it for what it was.

A shield.

She knew something. And she wasn't about to let him in on it.

Still, he couldn't demand answers now. He wanted her out of here. He didn't like the cabin's seclusion, the impenetrable wall of tall trees that surrounded it, the fact that he had no idea what, or who, might be hiding within those trees.

Most of all, he didn't like the fact that whoever had wanted to scare the bejeezus out of her had damned near done it. If she'd been alone when she saw that thing on the wall…

"Okay," he said, as he stood up, "the questions can wait."

"I'm not answering any questions, Mr. Orsini—but I have one for you. Exactly what are you doing here?"

"I see we're back to formalities."

"We're back to the fact that I didn't hire you as a bodyguard."

"Nobody hired me. I told you that. Consider me a volunteer."

"This is not a charity," she said coldly. "I don't accept volunteers."

Despite everything, he laughed. She didn't. She just fixed him with that look again. He figured it had surely sent other men running. Too bad she was wasting it on him.

"You followed me." Her tone was as sharp as a well-honed blade. "Why?"

He thought of taking her in his arms and giving her a graphic answer to the question, kissing her until she responded to him—and he could make that happen, he was certain—but it was a crazy idea. Besides, everything had to take a backseat to getting her the hell out of this place. They'd already been here too long.

Whoever had tacked that stuffed animal to the wall could still be outside. Okay, it was doubtful, but why take chances?

"Answer me, Mr. Orsini. Why did you follow me?"

"Maybe I like red VWs."

Elle rose to her feet. "Maybe I don't like smart answers."

"Look, baby—"

"Do not call me that!"

"Look, Ms. Bissette, you want conversation, fine. But not here."

"I am not the least bit interested in conversation. What I want are answers."

"So do I, but not here."

"On second thought, forget the answers. All I want is you out of here."

Falco narrowed his eyes. "Is it me, or do you just like giving men a tough time?"

"I don't give men anything," she snapped. "Why would I?"

Why, indeed. Was she into women? No way. That kiss in the desert assured him of that. Was she a woman who used men to suit her purposes, then discarded them when it was time for a change? Did she change lovers as often as some women changed hair color?

Not that it mattered. He had nothing to do with her life. Somebody was out to get this woman. The obscenity of it was not just wrong, it was vicious.

"Look," he said, trying hard to sound reasonable, "you can't stay here."

She laughed. It made his fists clench.

"Did I say something amusing?" he said.

"I don't know how to break this to you, Mr. Orsini, but I can do whatever I want."

"Somebody broke into your cabin. Left you a—a message."

"Oh, please! Break-ins happen in wild country like this. It was vandalism. Kids, plain and simple."

Falco smiled thinly. "Did kids nail that toy to the wall and send you that marked-up advertisement, too?"

It was a low blow. He knew it, wanted to feel guilty about it but if it forced her to see reality, it was worth it. He waited for her to retaliate. To his surprise, she didn't. Instead, she swung away from him, wrapped her arms around herself, and that did it. Falco clasped her shoulders and turned her toward him.

"Don't you see, Elle? These two things must be related."

She shook her head. "No," she whispered, "they aren't."

"And the sun won't set in the west."

She swallowed hard. "That's different."

"Yeah, it is. The sun isn't interested in hurting you."

For a few seconds, nothing happened. Then her eyes filled with darkness. "Oh, God," she whispered, "God…"

Falco muttered an obscenity, reached for her and gathered her close against him. A sob broke from her throat and he cupped her face, lifted it to his.

"I'll protect you," he said softly. "I swear it."

"I don't need anyone to protect me," she said, her voice breaking, and instead of arguing and telling her she was wrong, he drew her to him again and held her.

She felt warm and soft against him; the fragrance of her skin and hair was delicate and clean. He wanted to kiss her. Undress her. Take her to bed. Make love to her until she forget fear, forgot sorrow, until he was all that mattered.

Carefully, he cupped her shoulders, took a step back, waited until her eyes met his. Her nose was red and running. It made him want to hold her close again. Instead, he reached into his pocket, took out a pristine white handkerchief and handed it to her.

"Thank you," she said, and mopped her eyes, blew her nose. He nodded.

"So. I'm assuming you don't live here full-time."

"I don't, no."

"Is this a rental?"

"It's mine." Her voice was low; he had to strain to hear it. "I bought it with my first big paycheck."

"From that lingerie company?"

Damn, he hadn't meant to sound accusatory. What did he care if she smiled and pouted for the eyes of every man on the planet? But she simply nodded and said yes, that was right.

"I'd always wanted a place like this. Quiet. Tucked away."

The cabin was definitely both. Still, someone had found it. A lover she'd brought here one weekend? The very possibility made him furious. That a man would violate a woman with such calculated cruelty. That a man would violate this particular woman—

Falco frowned. He was wasting precious time.

"Okay," he said briskly, "here's the plan. Get together anything you think you'll want. We'll leave your car. I'll arrange to have—"

"No." Elle shook off his hands. No more tears. No shaky voice. She was the portrait of composure.

"No, what? Your car will be fine. I'll arrange to have somebody pick it up and—"

"I'm not leaving."

"Dammit, woman, be reasonable."

"I'm being totally reasonable. If anybody—if anybody had wanted to—to do anything to me, they'd have been here, waiting."

"That's one way to look at it."

"It's the only way to look at it."

It wasn't, but telling her about similar situations that had ended in blood and disaster wasn't on the agenda right now. She thought she was being reasonable? Okay. He'd appeal to that.

"Look, there's nothing complicated about this, okay? Pick a friend. I'll drive you there and you can spend the night."

"I don't have friends."

His eyebrows rose. She made the announcement without drama, the way another woman might say she didn't have a potted geranium.

"It doesn't have to be a bosom buddy. Just somebody who'll put you up until tomorrow while I check things out."

Her expression went from composed to icy.

"Have I asked you to, as you so brilliantly put it, 'check things out' for me, Mr. Orsini?"

"Dammit, woman—"

"No. I have not. That's because I am perfectly capable of making my own plans."

"Then make some." Falco narrowed his eyes. "Otherwise I'll make them for you."

"You are an arrogant man, Mr. Orsini. That may impress some of your clients but it doesn't do a thing for me."

"I don't have 'clients,'" Falco said, each word dipped in ice. "And if there's anybody here who's arrogant, baby, it's not me."

"My name is not 'baby.' And I am not going to explain myself to you."

Forget arrogant, forget determined. Her tone, her posture, the look on that gorgeous face was downright hostile.

"I have a car. If I want to go somewhere, I'll drive myself."

"Fine. You take the VW. I'll follow you."

"Are you hard of hearing, Mr. Orsini? I'm staying right here."

The hell she was, Falco thought grimly. She was not staying here—and neither was he. It was too late, too dark to check the woods. Somebody was stalking her; why she refused to acknowledge that was a question that needed answering but he'd screwed around here much, much longer than was prudent.

And he wasn't about to waste more time arguing with a woman who gave new meaning to the word *mulish*.

"Don't you get it, Mr. Orsini? You are dismissed."

That did it. Falco scooped Elle Bissette off her feet and dumped her over his shoulder. She was an egotistical, irritating, obstinate witch, but no way would he leave her in a place like this.

She punched, kicked, shrieked. None of it mattered. He walked straight through the cabin, along the dirt track to the road, right to where he'd left the SUV, its ebony surface lit by a newly risen ivory moon.

"Son of a bitch," Elle huffed. "You no-good, no-account—"

"Do us both a favor," Falco said, "and shut up." He shifted her weight, yanked open the passenger door and dumped her in the black leather seat. She responded by trying to scramble out, but he'd expected that and he put one big hand in the center of her chest and unceremoniously shoved her back. "Stay put," he warned, "or so help me, I'll tie you up and stuff you in the cargo compartment."

She looked up at him, starlit eyes hot with fury.

"You bastard! For all I know you—you pinned that—that thing to the wall in there."

Okay. She knew he hadn't but the look on his handsome, arrogant face was worth the stupid taunt.

"Right." His voice dripped with sarcasm. "I figured out where you were heading, got here before you, hung kitty up, drove away, hid out and waited until you arrived." His mouth twisted. "Man, I am one clever dude!"

"You have no right to—to kidnap me."

He laughed. Laughed, damn him, as if she and the entire situation were amusing.

"Is that what you're going to tell the cops? You are one lucky lady. I mean, two chances to call the cops in one day?" His laughter died; his voice turned cold and he leaned down until their eyes were almost level. "Go on, baby. Use your mobile. Call the cops, tell them how you found that message in your cabin—"

"What message?" she said and, once again, her words tumbled out too fast.

"Oh, it was a message, all right. We both know that. The difference is, I don't understand it—but I have a feeling you sure as hell do."

Her chin lifted. "That's ridiculous."

"Good. So call them. Tell them what you found, tell them how I dragged you out of the freaking middle of freaking nowhere to save your pretty ass. Tell them that's what you call a kidnap, and I'll stick around for the laughs."

Pay dirt. He could see it, see the fight drain out of her.

"Bastard," she hissed.

"If only," Falco said with a quick, dangerous smile.

"I hate you!"

"And that breaks my heart."

"It couldn't. You have no heart, Orsini."

"I've been told that before."

"Oh, yes, I'll just bet you have."

Her mouth was trembling, that soft-looking mouth. He remembered the taste of it, the hint of sweetness she had not given him time to savor and then he thought, what the hell, she might as well hate him for cause and he leaned in, captured that sweet mouth with his, kissed her, swept his hands into her hair when she tried to turn away…

And heard the soft catch of her breath, the whisper of acquiescence that told him all he needed to know.

The need burning hot inside him burned inside her, too.

"Elle," he said, and her lips softened. Parted. Clung to his.

He said her name again and she moaned, curled her hands around his wrists as he took the kiss deeper and deeper.

The world fell away.

He could have her.

Everything in him knew it, knew as well that having her would be like nothing he'd ever known before. There had been women all his life but there'd never been a woman like this.

All he had to do was lift her from the SUV, carry her back into the cabin, undress her, bare her to his hands, his eyes, his mouth, take her again and again until he stripped her of that cold arrogance...

An owl hooted from the forest.

Falco pulled back.

Elle's eyes opened.

They were pools of deepest, darkest amber, shining with bewilderment. He could hardly blame her. Kissing her, wanting her, made no sense.

Neither did leaning in and kissing her again, his lips featherlight on hers.

"I'm in charge," he said in a low voice. "I'll take care of you. Nothing will happen to you, Elle, I swear it."

Then he slammed the door shut, went around to the driver's side, got behind the wheel and took the SUV away from the cabin fast enough to make dust rise into the moonlight.

CHAPTER SIX

THE NIGHT was magnificent, the ebony sky shot with silver starfire, the cool air fragrant with the tang of pine and fir.

The isolation, the beauty of the coastal mountains and the ever-present sound of the Pacific, beating against a rocky beach, were what had drawn Elle here in the first place.

In some ways, it reminded her of home and her earliest, happiest memories. No ocean, of course. She had grown up in a secluded valley hundreds and hundreds of miles from anything, least of all the sea. It had been a wonderful place, a wonderful life….

And then it had ended.

Elle frowned.

Why think of that now? She hadn't, for years. Until a few weeks ago. Until the ad torn from the fashion magazine…

"Are you cold?"

Startled, she turned to Falco Orsini.

"What?"

"You were shivering. If you're cold—"

"No. No, I'm fine. I just…" She bit her lip. "I'm fine," she said again, and looked down at her hands, tightly knotted in her lap.

Why had she let him carry her off? He'd given her little

choice, but the truth was, she could have stopped him.
Could have made the attempt to stop him, anyway. But she
hadn't. She'd let this stranger stuff her into the SUV and
drive away with her.

And she'd let him kiss her.

Elle closed her eyes against the unwanted memory. She'd
let him kiss her, force a response from her...

Liar!

He hadn't "forced" anything. He'd put his lips on hers and
something had happened deep inside her, something she had
never believed could possibly happen if a man kissed her.

But it had.

She'd kissed him back, kissed him and wanted to go on
kissing him.

Which only proved what bad shape she was in.

She did not respond to—to that kind of thing. Why would
she? She knew women did but she'd never been able to
understand it. And what impression had she made with that
one moment of irrational behavior? Did the man beside her
think she would repay him for coming to her rescue by
having sex with him?

Not that he'd come to her rescue.

He'd turned up, unwanted, uninvited. Not once. Twice. In
the trailer. At the cabin. Yes, she'd flown into his arms when
he'd burst through the door but she'd have been fine if he
hadn't been there. She'd have gotten over her fear.

She would have.

Absolutely, she would have.

"Elle. If you're cold, just say so."

"I told you, I'm—"

He reached out, touched a button. The windows went up;
a whisper of warm air drifted through the vehicle. He
looked at her.

"Is that better?"

It was, actually. She hadn't realized it until now but he was right, she felt chilly.

"Yes. Thank you."

He nodded. Looked back at the windshield.

More silence.

They'd been driving for the better part of an hour, virtually alone on the narrow road. She'd never been on it this far past her cabin, hadn't even been curious where it led. Falco had turned onto it going fast, no signal light, checking and rechecking the mirrors. After a while, he'd settled into a steady, what, sixty, seventy miles an hour? They'd seen only two other vehicles, both heading toward them and then, a little while ago, headlights had come up behind them.

Falco had known it well before she did. She knew because she'd been watching him from the corner of her eye. That hard, handsome profile. The long fingers of one hand splayed over the steering wheel, the others lying loose on the gearshift lever.

Both hands had suddenly tightened.

A long minute later, the pinprick of headlights had illuminated the interior.

Logic told her his eyesight was better than hers. Instinct told her it had nothing to do with eyesight. He had sensed the presence of the other vehicle. He was like a predator, sleek and alert to every nuance of what might be prey, or what might prey on him.

Such a breathless analogy from a woman not given to breathless analogies, but she suspected it was accurate. Falco Orsini was different. At this point, nothing about him could surprise her.

Well, yes, she thought. Something could. Or, rather, something had. The way he'd kissed her.

The way she'd responded.

Back to that.

Elle turned her face to the window and stared blindly into the night. She responded to music. To art. That didn't come close to describing how she had reacted to that kiss. The quick, reflexive sense of disgust. Of revulsion. The shock at the feel of a man's mouth on hers…

And then, oh, God, and then the incredible explosion of heat that had swept through her thighs, her belly, her breasts…

"Take the ramp, on right, in four-point-eight miles."

Startled, Elle swung toward him. "What was that?"

"My navigator."

"Your what?"

"My navigator," he repeated. "She says we turn off just ahead."

Was she losing her mind? "Who says?"

Falco flashed a quick grin. It was so unexpected that she was half-afraid her mouth had dropped open.

"The GPS," he said, jerking his chin toward the dashboard. "The Voice of the Robot Queen. She has all the charm of a machine but she's generally right on the money."

The global positioning system. Of course. Elle looked at the lighted panel. Was she so far gone that she hadn't noticed it glowing like a TV monitor?

"I turned it on only a few minutes ago," Falco said, as if he'd read her thoughts. "I don't know this area and I don't want to just keep driving without doing some reconnoitering."

"Reconnoitering?" she said blankly.

"Checking things out. Making some plans."

"What plans? As soon as we get to Los Angeles—"

"Is that where you live?"

"In Studio City. Yes. The street is—"

"We're not going there."

Elle cocked her head. "What do you mean, we're not going there?"

Falco shifted his weight. "I told you before. I want you someplace safe."

"And I told you—"

"Turn right in point-three miles."

"I know what you told me." Lights glowed faintly in the distance ahead; a sign flashed by. The name of a town she'd never heard of, logos for food, for gas, for motels. "Remember? I asked if you had a friend who'd take you in for the night and you told me that you didn't."

He was right. He'd asked and she, idiot that she was, had stupidly said she had no friends. It was true enough but she hadn't meant he could take her wherever it was he was taking her.

"Look, Mr. Orsini—"

"I'd think, after all this, we could give up the 'Mister' thing, don't you?"

She looked at him, felt the rush of color climb her face until she realized he hadn't meant the remark the way she'd taken it. His tone was level, his concentration still on the road. He'd been referring to what had happened in the cabin, not to the kiss.

The kiss hadn't meant anything to him. Why would it? He'd probably kissed more women than he could remember. She wasn't a fool, she knew that most women would be eager to be kissed by a man like him.

She also knew the reason he'd kissed her. To show control. He'd even told her that. Not that it had been necessary. She knew all about that kind of thing.

The SUV slowed, took a right.

"Pick one."

Bewildered, she swung toward him. "One what?"

"A motel. Your choice." He slowed the SUV and now

she saw the line of motels fronting what had become a four-lane road.

Her belly knotted.

What she'd feared was happening. He had taken that kiss as permission to take her. A bitter taste filled her mouth. Despite everything she knew about men, a tiny part of her had hoped he was different.

She should have known better.

None of them were different, she thought coldly, and sat up straight in the leather seat.

"Forget it," she snapped.

"Yeah, I know. They're not up to your usual standards but it's the best we're going to do."

"You've miscalculated, Mr. Orsini."

Her voice was cold enough to turn water to ice. What now? Falco thought wearily. He was bone tired; the last thing he wanted was another battle.

"Look," he said, "it's late. I told you, I don't know this area. I punched in a request for a place to stay the night, the GPS came up with this as the closest loc—"

"I am not sleeping with you."

Her tone was quick and sharp. Another time, another place, he might have seen her reaction as having some logic to it. She was a movie star; she was paid to turn men on. Maybe that was a crude way to put it, but, basically, it was what women like her did. He was a stranger, a man who had shown up, uninvited, in her life and now he'd told her they were going to spend the night at a cheap motel.

So, yes, maybe her attitude bore some semblance of logic.

Unfortunately, he wasn't in the mood to see it.

For starters, he didn't like Elle Bissette. She was a gorgeous package on the outside, but on the inside, she was the worst kind of snob. She'd taken one look at him and decided he wasn't in her league. He despised that kind of thinking; he'd never be interested in a woman who made judgments like that, not even for a night's worth of sex with a woman most men would crawl over each other to reach.

Besides, sex was the last thing on his mind.

He was tired and hungry and what he wanted was a shower, a hot meal, enough strong coffee to keep him awake while she told him what in hell was going on because, come hell or high water, she was going to tell him.

Then he wanted to fall into bed and sleep.

And all Elle Bissette could think of was that he was going to jump her bones?

Anger rose inside him, quick and hot. At her, at himself. He slammed on the brakes and pulled into the parking lot of the nearest motel, stopping the engine and swinging toward her even as he did.

"Has anybody ever told you that you have one incredibly overblown idea of where you stand on the desirability scale?"

Elle undid her seat belt and reached for the door handle. "Good night, Mr. Orsini. It's been—"

Falco's hand wrapped around her elbow. He spun her toward him.

"You really think that's what this is all about? That I took one look at the famous Elle Bissette and began plotting a way I could get my hands on her?"

Color shot into her face. "You're disgusting!"

"Or maybe you think that's the way I get women into my bed. Wander around, find one who looks as if she needs a little help, then tell her she owes me."

"Let go of my arm!"

"Well, let me set the record straight. I'm not interested. Have you got that, or you want it spelled out?"

"Damn you! I said—"

"I heard what you said." Falco, eyes glinting, mouth hard, leaned forward. "You are nothing I would ever want."

"And nothing you could ever have!"

"You don't get it. A man would have to be crazy to put up with an egotistical psycho like you."

"Thank you for the personality analysis," she said coldly. "Be sure and add the cost to your bodyguarding bill."

"Trust me, honey." Falco's lips twisted. "My services cost nothing. The whole thing is free of charge."

"Fine, because that's exactly what your services are worth."

"I'd sooner go to bed with a block of ice than with you."

She flashed an ice-queen smile. "Whatever turns you on, Orsini."

"Not you, babe, that's for sure."

Elle recoiled. His words were like a slap in the face and that was ridiculous. She had no wish to turn anybody on, certainly not a man like him, all that overbearing arrogance, that swaggering masculinity...

All that strength, the courage, the sudden hints at tenderness...

Qualities he didn't have, she thought grimly. Qualities she'd assigned him because she had the imagination that went with being an actress.

Elle raised her chin. "Are you done?"

"I'm done, all right." Falco lifted his hand from her arm. "You want out?"

"Damned right I do."

"Fine." He dug in his pocket, hauled out his wallet. "You'll need cash."

"I won't need anything from you."

"Yeah, you will. Or did you remember to grab your purse before I hauled you out of that cabin?"

That stopped her. Her eyes narrowed.

"Hauled me out, is right. Carrying me out of there as if—as if I were a recalcitrant child."

Dammit, how could she do this? How could she accuse him of being the worst kind of bastard? And how could she be so beautiful?

Her eyes blazed. Her mouth was set in a sulky pout. She was full of passion and life and no matter what he thought of her, the fact that some crazy wanted to hurt her made his belly knot.

"Exactly as if I were a recalcitrant child, if you even know what the word means!"

"That's enough." His voice was low, rough, filled with warning.

"You think you can—you can pretend you want to protect me when all the while, all the while you just want to—to overpower me—"

"Elle." He grasped her wrists. "You know better than that."

"Oh, I know better, all right. I know all about men like you…"

Her voice broke. Falco was looking at her as if she were crazy and perhaps she was. Everything he'd said was true. He'd done nothing but offer her kindness and she—and she—

Tears rose in her eyes and spilled down her cheeks. Falco cursed and reached for her. She gave a little mew of protest, but when he pulled her into his arms, she burrowed against him.

"I didn't mean—"

"I know." And he did know; she was terrified and doing one hell of a job of not showing it. Beautiful as well as brave, he thought, and drew her closer.

"I just— Everything seems so out of control—"

"It isn't," he said with more conviction than he felt. "You're safe and I'm going to keep you that way."

She gave a wet sniffle. "I know you didn't bring me here to—to seduce me."

"No," he said, trying for a light touch as he held her, rocked her gently in his arms. "I'm more a hot sheet motel man myself."

She gave a hiccupping laugh. It was a start. He went on rocking her, his lips pressed lightly to her hair. It smelled of the night and, incongruously, of roses. After a few seconds, she lifted her head from his shoulder. "Falco?"

"Yeah?"

"I know—I know you didn't bring me here looking for—for payment."

"Damned right, I didn't," he said gruffly.

"But—but you have the right to know that—that it isn't you. I mean, I'm just not— I'm just not—"

"That's okay," he said, and wondered why the words sounded hollow. A few seconds went by. Then he cleared his throat. "Is it that make-believe cowboy actor?"

"Chad?" Elle gave a low laugh. "He's got a wife he's crazy about and six kids. No. It's not him. It's just—it's just that I don't do that."

"Sleep around." Why did that admission make him feel so damned good? "I'm glad."

"No. I mean—I mean, I don't—I don't do the—the sex thing."

She felt a stillness suddenly settle over him. What in the world had made her make such an admission? Sex was not something she thought about, much less talked about, not in any way, not with anyone.

"The sex thing," he said, as if he'd never heard those words before.

Elle winced. What he'd never heard were those three words infused with such special meaning. How could she have shown such little discretion? Irritation at herself made her tone turn cool.

"Is that a problem?"

Yes, Falco thought, it damned well was. That a woman should not like sex, because that had to be what not "doing" the sex thing meant, that a woman, especially one who looked like this, who felt warm and soft in a man's arms, whose mouth tasted of honey, should feel that way about sex was, well, unfortunate.

But was it a problem for him?

No.

He was, okay, attracted to her. Never mind all that stuff he'd told himself a little while ago. She was incredibly easy on the eyes and she needed help.

His help.

Whatever mess she was in had *Danger* written all over it. That kind of thing upped the ante. A maiden in distress. A knight on a white charger, and never mind how tarnished his armor might be. Add it all together and you had a hot thing going.

Hell, he'd been there enough times to know.

But there were other women. There would always be other women. That was the cold, honest, down-and-dirty truth. Women liked to think the world was full of kindred souls searching for each other.

Men knew better.

He did, anyway.

At seventeen, he'd made out with Cathy Callahan in the backseat of her father's Buick. A month later, Cathy was history and he'd repeated the performance with Angie Baroni under the creaky stands of a high school on Staten Island where he'd won an "away" football game with a last-minute touchdown and she'd waved her pom-poms and cheered.

Of course, he'd polished his style over the ensuing years but even his brothers, no one man/one woman forever enthusiasts themselves—though that seemed to have changed recently for Dante and Rafe—had laughed and said it would be a day at the beach in Antarctica when Falco Orsini decided he needed one woman to the exclusion of all others.

"Mr. Orsini?"

Falco frowned, focused on the lovely and suddenly composed face inches from his.

"Just in case you see this as a challenge to your masculinity…"

Her voice had become cool. It irritated him, the sudden change from tender to tough, but, hell, he admired it, too.

For a couple of seconds, he wondered how she'd react if he said yes, that was exactly how he saw it, that she'd melted in his arms a little while ago and was he really expected to believe she wasn't in to, as she put it, "the sex thing"?

But none of this was about sex. It was about keeping her safe.

That was all that mattered.

Time to lighten the mood again, he decided. He put a serious look on his face and drew back. She sat up straight, her eyes wary as they met his.

"Here's my best offer," he said politely. "You stop calling me 'Mr. Orsini,' I'll try and survive the blow to my ego. How's that sound?" He almost laughed at the expression on her face. Clearly, his answer was not what she'd expected. "Deal?" he said, holding out his hand.

He watched her think it over. Then she gave a quick smile and put her hand in his. "Deal."

And just the brush of her palm against his, the touch of her fingers, made every muscle in his body leap to attention.

Something told him celibacy wasn't going to be as easy as he'd made it sound.

He left her in the SUV while he got them a room.

The clerk must have been asleep. He showed up at the desk

looking bleary-eyed. Falco signed the register as E. Presley, 10 Blue Suede Lane, Memphis, Tennessee, and ignored the line where you were supposed to enter your license plate number. He didn't mention there was anyone else with him, paid cash, took the room key card—he suspected it would turn out to be the most up-to-date feature in the place—and asked if there was somewhere nearby to get a meal.

"Diner's one block that direction," the clerk said, smothering a yawn.

Falco nodded, thanked the guy and strolled out to the parking lot. Elle was still there. She was sound asleep, her head resting on the seat back.

He got behind the wheel and watched her for a couple of minutes. She looked exhausted, incredibly young…and there it was again, that sweet vulnerability that had brought him to Hollywood in the first place.

A muscle knotted in his jaw.

He drove to the rear of the two-story building. He'd requested a corner room on the first floor and the parking space directly in front of it was empty. Most of the spaces were; it didn't take much effort to figure out that the world had long-ago bypassed this little town.

He got out of the SUV, went around to the passenger door, opened it.

"Elle."

Nothing. Not even a flutter of her lashes.

"Elle," he said more loudly, "come on, wake up. We'll get washed, then go get something to eat and have a long talk." He sighed. "Okay, we can talk tomorrow. Showers, food, and then you can climb into a real bed."

Still nothing. Falco leaned into the car, touched her shoulder.

"Elle, come on. Open your eyes."

She murmured something and turned her face toward him. Her hair brushed over his fingers. Her breath caressed his cheek. The muscle in his jaw knotted again. Okay. Let her sleep. He'd carry her into the motel room, give her a few minutes, then wake her.

Lifting her was simple. One arm under her, the other around her. He stepped away from the car, kicked the door shut. It was easy enough to shift her weight, carry her to the room and maneuver the key card into the lock. The door opened to a dark room that smelled of disinfectant and disuse. He used his elbow to feel around for a wall switch, found one and hit it.

A dull light came on.

The room was small, shabby but clean. The furnishings were utilitarian. One window. One chair.

One double bed.

Her carried her to it, stood her on her feet while he kept one arm clamped tightly around her. She slumped against him like a rag doll as he drew back the patterned bedspread, pulled down the thin top sheet and equally thin blanket.

"Come on, baby," he said softly. Slowly, gently, he eased her down on the mattress.

She gave a deep sigh. So deep, he thought, so weary. It was a sigh of exhaustion.

He took off her shoes. Thought about taking off her clothes and getting her down to her underwear and just as quickly decided against it. Instead, he pulled up the covers, tucked them around her shoulders, all his movements brisk and businesslike…

Yeah, but brisk and businesslike didn't keep him from thinking of how much he wanted to bend down and brush her lips with his. Just that. A light kiss. A way to repeat his pledge to keep her safe.

"Hell," he muttered.

He checked the window lock, pulled the curtain. Double-locked the door. Located the heating unit and turned it to high.

Okay. To the john next. He used the facilities, washed his hands, his face, tore open the plastic pack that held a plastic cup, filled it with a tepid mix of water and chlorine from the tap and rinsed his mouth. It wasn't the best hygiene in the world but it would have to do.

In the bedroom again, he turned out the light, waited a few seconds until his eyes adjusted to the dark. The single chair looked as if it might support a dwarf but not a man who stood six-three. And the last time he'd weighed himself at the gym near the Orsini Brothers Investments building in Manhattan, he'd been at 220.

There was always the floor, but he needed a night's rest.

"Okay," he said, as if there were someone there to hear him.

Falco toed off his mocs and lay down on the bed as far from Elle as he could. The mattress sagged, the heater was making noise though it wasn't producing much heat, but he'd slept in places that made this look like a palace.

Elle Bissette, Hollywood actress, surely had not. That cabin she owned wasn't luxurious by any means but she'd made it clear it had sentimental value to her as her first big purchase.

Her day-to-day home, in L.A., was certain to be movie-star impressive.

Shabby motel room or not, she had not awakened. But she'd started dreaming, making little noises, arms and legs twitching. Not a good dream, whatever it was.

"Elle," he said softly. "You're okay."

She whimpered. Her lovely face contorted.

The hell with it.

Falco moved closer and gathered her in his arms, whispering reassurances. He felt the tension ease from her body. After a minute or two she sighed, turned toward him and lay her head on his shoulder, her hand over his heart. Her breathing went from choppy to relaxed.

He told himself he could let go of her now.

He could…

But he didn't. Instead, he drew her closer. Shut his eyes as he inhaled the clean, sweet fragrance of her skin.

And followed her into sleep.

CHAPTER SEVEN

ELLE CAME awake slowly, rising from the depths of a deep, dreamless sleep.

It was the first time in longer than she could remember that she hadn't spent the night trapped within fragmented dream landscapes…

Unless she was dreaming right now.

She felt the sudden leap of her heart.

Yes. This had to be a dream. How else to explain coming awake in a strange bed in a strange room, the half light of dawn visible behind the curtain?

How else to explain coming awake in the warm, strong arms of a man?

"Morning," a husky male voice murmured into her hair, and Elle knew it wasn't a dream at all.

Frantic, she tried to pull free of Falco's embrace. That didn't work. His arms only tightened around her.

"Don't panic," he said softly. "It's me. Falco."

If that was supposed to calm her, it didn't. Elle's struggles increased.

"Elle," he said quietly, "we shared the bed, that's all. Nothing happened. Absolutely nothing."

They'd shared the bed. Shared a night's rest. Elle stopped struggling, took a long breath.

"We're both still fully dressed." His words took on a touch of light humor. "If we'd done anything except sleep, trust me, honey, we wouldn't be."

He was right. She was wearing all her clothes. So was he. But his arms were around her... His arms were around her, and she was safe.

Elle let out a breath and went still in his embrace.

"Okay?"

She nodded and slowly, carefully, looked up at him. Her heart gave another leap but it had nothing to do with fear. What a beautiful man he was! Instinct told her he'd laugh at hearing himself described that way but it was true. His face had the elegant bone structure of Michelangelo's *David*: the strong nose, chiseled lips, firm jaw. His eyes were very dark, all obsidian pupils in the dusky early morning light; his lashes were long and enviably thick.

Beautiful, indeed.

The night had brought the shadow of morning stubble to his cheeks. Male models often cultivated that look to give them a macho aura but it never quite worked.

It did on Falco Orsini.

He looked masculine and beautiful and dangerous.

And sexy. Incredibly sexy. It was just a reasonable conclusion. A woman didn't have to like sex to admit a man looked sexy.

"What are you thinking?"

Falco had a little smile on his lips. It was intimate and knowing, as if he'd read her thoughts, and it brought a rush of color to her cheeks.

"Nothing," she said quickly. "I mean—I mean, I was trying to remember what happened last night. The last thing I can recall, we were sitting in the car."

"Yeah." He caught a strand of her hair in his hand, let it

trail through his fingers. Her hair felt like silk. How could a woman look so beautiful after what she'd gone through last night, and without a drop of makeup? For years, he'd joked about what he called the 5:00 a.m. face, the one he swore women put on while a man was still sleeping rather than let him see her as she really was. This, what he saw now, was Elle's true five-in-the-morning face and it was spectacular. Skin as creamy as satin. Eyes bright with intelligence. Cheekbones washed with light color. And that mouth. That lovely mouth, so pink, so soft, so perfect…

Falco forced himself to breathe normally, dragged his thoughts away from entering what could only be dangerous territory.

"I left you in the SUV, booked this room…" He smiled. "When I got back, you were sound asleep. So I carried you inside." He smiled again. "You missed your chance to get a first look at our deluxe, six-star accommodations. Does that do it?" He could see that it didn't. "No, huh? You're wondering what you're doing here, in bed with me."

She felt her face fill with heat. Falco nodded.

"Well, it never occurred to me to ask the character in the front office what the sleeping arrangements were. Turned out we have only the one bed. I put you on it. Then I looked around and saw that I had a couple of options. I could sack out on the Aubusson on the floor—"

Okay. That had helped. Elle's lips curved in a smile. It was faint, but yes, it was a smile.

"Definitely an Aubusson," she said.

"My other option was that very comfortable Eames chair."

She peeped over his shoulder. Eames, indeed. The battered chair reminded her of one in a shelter where she and her mother had once stayed. Something of the memory must have shown on her face because Falco put his hand under her chin and tilted her face to his.

"Hey," he said softly, "are you okay?"

"Yes, of course." She forced a smile. "Lucky man, to have had two such great choices."

He grinned. "I thought so, too. That's why I went for option numero three. Share the bed by taking the far side of it." His smile faded; his eyes turned dark again. "But you started dreaming. It didn't take much to see it wasn't a good dream so I got you out of it and you sort of turned toward me and I figured if I pushed you away you'd fall back into that dream so I stayed where I was and you—you settled in."

She wanted to tell him she didn't believe him, that she'd never, as he'd called it, "settled in" a man's arms and never would. But his tone was calm, his gaze steady. And the way they were lying, she in his arms, her hand on his heart, was proof that he was telling the truth.

How could she feel safe with this man? With any man, but especially one this big, this strong, this sure of himself?

He was watching her with an intensity that would have sent her running just twenty-four hours ago, but now—

Now, she found herself wondering what the stubble on his jaw would feel like under the brush of her fingers. Would it be bristly or soft? She could find out in a second. All she had to do was lift her hand, touch his face and then—then, maybe that tingle in her breasts, her belly would go away.

"Elle."

His voice was low. Rough. The sound of it thrilled her.

"Baby. You keep looking at me like that and—"

She knew what she had to do. Stop looking at him. Move away. Get up from the bed.

"And what?" she said in a voice she hardly recognized as her own.

Falco groaned, bent his head and kissed her. It was the lightest of kisses, just the soft brush of his lips over hers.

And it wasn't enough.

She heard the sharp intake of her own breath and then her hands were lifting, lifting, moving up his chest, over his shoulders, capturing his face and yes, oh, yes, that stubble on his cheeks felt incredible. Soft, like his mouth. Rough, like his voice when he'd said her name.

He said it again now, whispered it against her mouth, and then he groaned and rolled her onto her back, came down over her, cupped her face as she was cupping his and his lips moved against hers, his kiss changed, hungry now, hot and wild and she yielded to it, more than yielded, wanted it, wanted his kiss, wanted him.

She moaned and flung her leg over his. He made a rough sound, slid his hand under her shirt, cupped her breast. A cry broke from her throat. She put her hand over his, felt her nipple swelling, beading, felt a liquid heat forming low in her belly…

Felt a wave of sheer terror sweep through her.

"No!"

Her cry of fear was fierce. She tore her mouth from Falco's and at first she thought he wasn't going to let go of her but then his big, hard body went still and he rolled away from her and got to his feet.

Silence filled the dingy room. She wanted to say something, anything. But he spoke first.

"It's getting late," he said brusquely. "I want to be out of here ASAP."

Elle scrambled up against the creaking headboard. Falco's mouth was a flat line, his eyes were cold. She knew she owed him an explanation but how could she offer one when she couldn't even explain what had happened to herself?

"Falco, I'm sorry. I didn't mean to—to lead you on."

He looked straight at her. What she saw in his face made her breath catch.

"It was my mistake."

"No, it was me. I don't even understand why—"

"No," he said coldly, "neither do I. I'm responsible for your safety. I lost sight of that but it won't happen again." He swung away from her. "I'm going to take a shower. When I'm done, you can do the same."

"Falco…"

"Five minutes," he said curtly. "Then we're out of here."

He was impossible.

Caring one minute, unfeeling the next.

She knew she'd hurt him. Not him. His pride. She'd had a couple of minutes to think and she was pretty sure she knew what had happened. She was frightened, she'd reacted in the most primitive way to a primitive man.

No. Falco was a lot of things but "primitive" wasn't one of them despite the long, muscular body, the quick reflexes, the ability to think and react like a predator.

And he wasn't a man who'd take advantage of a woman's emotions.

He wouldn't have to.

Elle took her turn in the bathroom. She stood under the lukewarm spray—that was as hot as the water would get—and wondered what twist of fate had sent him into her life. The better question was, how would she get him out of it?

That arrogant declaration. *I'm responsible for your safety.* The hell he was! Nobody was responsible for anything about her except her.

Was that true? What about what she'd found waiting at the cabin last night? What if Falco hadn't been there to take her in his arms and ease her terror?

She shut her eyes, lifted her face to the tepid spray.

The toy cat had frightened her more than the marked-up Bon Soir ad, more than the note, more than anything she could have anticipated. The toy cat, her toy or one that was its absolute image, pinned to the wall of a cabin nobody knew existed except her…

Ever since this started, she'd told herself she didn't know the reason for it or who could do this to her. A lie. She knew. At least, she had a very good idea. And she could no longer avoid admitting it to herself, but, dear heaven, not to anyone else.

A fist banged on the bathroom door. "One minute, Bissette. After that, we'll pass on breakfast."

Elle's eyes narrowed. Forget caring. Falco Orsini was a bullying dictator. She didn't want him poking his nose into her life. She couldn't afford to let him poke his nose into her life!

Once they returned to the real world from wherever this place was, she'd get rid of him. *Here's a check for your time, a handshake, and goodbye, Mr. Bodyguard.*

As for that ridiculous threat about passing on breakfast… Did he really think he could scare her with such nonsense?

Her stomach growled.

Elle rolled her eyes, shut off the water and reached for a towel.

Falco worried that someone might recognize her. Her face was famous. The last thing he wanted was to have word go out that Elle Bissette was in whatever in hell you called this town.

Once they were in the rented SUV, he grabbed the pair of sunglasses he'd left on the dash and handed them to her.

"Put them on," he said curtly.

She looked at them as if she'd never seen dark glasses before.

"I don't need them," she said, "but thank you for the offer."

He almost grinned. The thank-you was as close to being a four-letter word as anyone could have managed. The lady had balls, he had to give her credit for that.

"Put them on anyway."

"I just said—"

"You want a meal? Or you want some truck driver spotting the famous Elle Bissette and calling the local news station?"

She glared at him, obviously hating that he'd out thought her. Then she snatched the glasses from his hand and plopped them on her nose.

Better, but not perfect.

Falco made a quick left and pulled in to a gas station. He pumped the tank full, went into the minuscule office to pay and came out with a red ball cap emblazoned with the oil company's logo.

"Put your hair up and wear this."

She looked at the cap, gave a little shudder—a shudder that would have been lots more dramatic had she seen the guy who'd been wearing the thing before Falco bought it for twenty bucks. But she twisted her hair into something like a ponytail, held it at the crown of her head, then pulled on the cap and yanked it low over her eyes.

Definitely better. You could still see her nose, her mouth and her chin, all delicate, all beautiful, all pure Elle Bissette, but he knew damned well that the only man who'd realize that was the one who'd held her in his arms through the night, who'd awakened long before she had and imagined what might happen if he woke the sleeping princess with a kiss.

He was a damned fool.

He stepped hard on the gas even though the diner was only a couple of hundred feet ahead and lurched into a parking slot.

"I know it's not what you're accustomed to," he said coldly, "but we all have to make sacrifices."

She shot him a look. "You have no idea what I'm accustomed to," she said, and before he could respond, tell her he damned well did and that third-rate motels, greasy-spoon diners and stuck-up females were not what he was accustomed to, either, she was out of the car and striding toward the door.

What had happened this morning was what had to happen when a man woke up tenting the sheets. Elle had been handy, that was all. He hadn't liked her from the start and the more time he spent with her, the more that assessment was validated.

As for that heart-wrenching little story about not "doing the sex thing"… Bull. What she did understand was how easy it was to use men. A little teasing, then pull back. It probably kept guys on the edge of sanity until she got things her own way.

She was almost at the front door. Falco went after her, grabbed her wrist, jerked her against his side.

"I can walk without your help, Orsini," she snapped.

"Not while you're with me," he snapped back, and the way she looked up at him said, as clearly as words, that being with him was a situation that wasn't going to go on much longer.

And that was just fine with him.

She didn't open the menu.

"I'm not hungry," she said and when the waitress showed up, she ordered coffee. Black.

"The house special," Falco said. "Do the eggs over easy, make sure the bacon's crisp. Hotcakes, not French toast, extra syrup on the side." He looked up at the girl and smiled. "Please."

Please was all it took, Elle thought coldly. The waitress's answering smile made it clear she'd have walked on burning coals to provide whatever this particular customer wanted.

"Toast?"

"Rye. And do the whole thing twice."

Elle waited until the girl hurried away. "I hope you didn't order the extra meal for me. I told you, I'm not—"

"Hungry. I'm not deaf. Just let the food sit there if you don't want it."

They waited in silence until the waitress brought their breakfasts, one gigantic platter for him, one for Elle. He spread a napkin in his lap, picked up his fork and dug in. He could feel Elle's eyes on him. After a couple of seconds, she put her napkin in her lap, too, and reached for her fork.

He raised an eyebrow. She flashed him a murderous look, but when she spoke, her voice was surprisingly young, almost childlike.

"It's a sin to let food go to waste."

Then she dug in.

She ate everything.

He wondered about that. Was it because she believed leaving it would have been wrong? Or was she starved for a solid meal? Despite what she obviously thought about him, Falco had dated a lot of models, a couple of actresses and a well-known Broadway star. All of them had moaned about having to watch their weight; they'd order endless courses, then poke at them.

Not Elle.

She ate as if it mattered. Then she slugged down two mugs of black coffee, made a quick trip to the ladies room and they were on their way again.

"Where are we going?"

"To your cabin."

"Good. I'll get my car—"

"I want to see if anyone's been there since we left. Assuming they didn't, you can pick up your handbag and anything else you can't do without. Then you're going to tell me where you live and we'll go there."

"That's ridiculous. I am perfectly capable—"

"That's how we're going to do it," he said in a take-no-prisoners tone. "You don't agree, we'll bypass the cabin and head straight for your place."

He felt her eyes on him. "I really dislike you intensely, Mr. Orsini."

Back to square one. "That breaks my heart."

"Such a childish attitude. Just because I didn't—I didn't succumb to your pathetic attempt at seduction…"

Elle gasped as Falco turned the wheel hard, brought the SUV to the shoulder of the road and shifted into Park.

"Is that what you think this is all about?"

"I know that's what this is all about."

"You seem to know everything you need to about me," he said coldly. "Well, here's a flash. I wasn't the one who started things this morning."

"Not true," she said, even as a small voice inside her said *He's right, it was all your doing.*

His smile made her wedge herself as far into the corner as her seat belt would permit. "You're good, I'll give you that. The dramatic little scene about not doing 'the sex thing'— and then, the next second, you're looking up at me with big, innocent eyes and asking me to make love to you—"

"I didn't do anything of the sort! I never asked you to—"

His fingers flew, undoing his seat belt, then hers, and he hauled her into his arms.

"Do you think that's the way to keep a guy like me in line?"

"What are you talking about?"

"Play that kind of game again, baby, I can promise you how it will end."

"No. It wasn't a—"

He kissed her, his lips taking hers, parting hers, possessing hers. She formed a hand into a fist, pounded it against his shoulder but he was ruthless, determined—and suddenly she felt fire ignite in her blood, felt it rush from her breasts to her belly.

Falco lifted his head.

"No more games," he said gruffly. "Not unless you're prepared to play straight to the end."

Calmly, as if nothing had happened, he closed the latch of her seat belt, then his, turned on the engine and pulled back onto the road.

The cabin stood silent, the door open as he'd left it and stirring idly in the soft breeze.

He could tell no one had been there since they'd left but he wasn't about to take chances. He took a long look before he opened the car door.

"Stay," he commanded.

Elle smiled sweetly. "Woof woof."

He couldn't help it. He laughed.

"Good girl," he said, and laughed again when she bared her teeth.

He checked the cabin. Nobody. Elle's purse and car keys were where she'd left them. He grabbed them, did another walk-through, then went back to the SUV.

"Has anyone…"

Her laughter was gone. Her eyes were big and filled with anxiety.

"No," he said. "The place is untouched."

She let out her breath. "That's good. That's very good. And since that's the case, Mr. Orsini—"

Falco raised his eyebrows.

"Since that's the case, Falco, you can surely leave me here."

"Forget that."

"I'm not going to stay." She shuddered. "I'm never going to stay here again. I'll just get into my car and drive myself home."

"To find what? Something similar to what you found here?"

"Oh, for God's sake," she said, no more dulcet tones wrapping the words in sugar, "I'll be absolutely fine!"

"That's the way it's going to be, Elle. I'll drive you to your place. Check it out. If everything's okay, I'll leave."

Her eyes searched his. "Promise?"

"Promise," he said, but why spoil things by adding that he'd first telephone a guy he knew out here who did excellent body-guard work because he wasn't about to leave Elle on her own and he sure as hell wasn't about to go on guarding her. He had a life to go back to. Anyone could do this job; it didn't have to be him. He didn't have to like his clients or whatever you wanted to call them, but he had to at least get along with them.

He and Elle were not getting along, that was for sure—especially in those moments when he crossed the line he always kept between himself and those who needed his help. He'd never done that, until now. And he didn't like it…

"Promise," he said again, and crossed his heart, but with his fingers crossed the way he and his brothers used to when they were kids lying to each other. "So, if there's anything you want inside…"

She hesitated. Then she nodded, her face expressionless. She stepped from the SUV and headed for the cabin. He started after her but she held up her hand.

"It's just one thing. I can handle it by myself."

He waited, leaning against the SUV, arms folded while she went up the porch steps and into the cabin. The "one thing" was probably a sack full of cosmetics. Or jewelry. Or clothes. Just because she wasn't wearing makeup or jewelry, just because she was dressed like a couple of million other American women her age didn't mean—

How wrong could a man be?

She came out of the cabin a minute later, a small silver-framed photo in her hand.

"That's it?" he said in disbelief.

"That's it," she said.

He had questions. A thousand questions. But the expression on her face—sorrow, distress, despair so profound it made him forget his anger—kept him from voicing them.

"Okay," he said, and because it was too late to think, he leaned down when she reached him and kissed her. It was a soft kiss. Tender. And, for just long enough to make his heart kick against his ribs, she fitted her lips to his and kissed him back.

Then she got into the SUV, put the picture in her purse, told him her address in L.A. as if nothing had just happened and they made the two-hour trip in silence.

She lived, as she'd already told him, in Studio City.

A condo. The area was pleasant, the building was well-maintained, but Falco knew something about property costs out here and though prices in this part of Los Angeles might be astronomical by the standards of the American heartland, it didn't have the feel of super-priced real estate.

He went in alone, left Elle in the car.

"Stay put," he warned, but this time, he didn't get a sarcastic "woof" in response. She seemed remote. Was it because of that kiss? Or was she hoping everything would be okay here?

Part of him wanted to think it was because he'd told her he'd be leaving and that she was anticipating that and wishing it wouldn't happen, which was ridiculous. They were like oil and water; besides, he had work waiting back East, a tough meeting Monday with a banker from Indonesia, lunch Tuesday with a contingent of money men from Zurich.

As soon as he'd finished checking the condo, he'd put in a call to a guy he'd served with. Rick lived out here, he was top-notch at what he did.

Elle would be well-protected.

Her place was small, just a living room, small dining room, kitchen and lavatory on the lower level, all of it spotless and undisturbed. The rooms were nicely furnished but walking into it was pretty much like walking into a high-end hotel suite.

Falco climbed the steps to the upper level. A bathroom. Fine. A small room that seemed to be a home office. Also fine. The last door had to open on Elle's bedroom…

"Merda!"

Someone had taken the place apart. Drawers had been flung open, the contents dumped on the pale birch floor. Clothes had been yanked from the hangers. Words, ugly words describing women, had been scrawled on the pristine walls in what he at first thought was blood, but when he touched it, was red paint.

Worst of all was Elle's bed. Someone had gone at it with something sharp. A knife. A big knife. Nothing else could have left such devastation behind…

"Omigod!"

Falco whirled around. Elle stood in the doorway, her face white.

"My God," she said, "my God, my God, my God—"

He went to her, scooped her into his arms, carried her down the stairs to the SUV, got inside with her on his lap, his lips against her hair, his hands sliding up and down her spine, whispering words of reassurance.

Her arms were tight around his neck. She was shaking, sobbing, repeating "Why? Why? Why?" like a litany.

"Shhh, baby," he said, his arms tightening around her, holding her, rocking her, wanting to turn back the clock so she would not see what someone had done as much as he wished he'd been here when it happened so he could have killed the bastard who had done it with his bare hands.

At last, her trembling stopped. She took a couple of deep, shaky breaths. He felt her heartbeat slow. "Elle," he said softly, framing her face with his hands, drawing back so he could look into her eyes. "Elle. Who did this, honey? Who wants to hurt you?"

Her lips parted. She started to speak. Then she made a sad little sound and buried her face against his throat.

"I can't stay here," she whispered.

Falco nodded. "No," he said calmly, "you can't."

"There's a—a hotel on—"

"You can't stay there, either."

He was not only calm, but he also was possessed by a deadly quiet. His brothers, anyone who'd ever had anything to do with him, would have recognized it.

"I told you, there's no one I can impose on."

"It wouldn't matter. I don't want you in L.A." His mouth thinned. "Hell, I don't want you in California."

"Falco. That sounds good but—"

"Hawaii," he said. "Hawaii's perfect."

Elle sat back, Falco's arms enclosing her. She gave what might have been a laugh.

"Hawaii is six hours away. I've never been there. I don't know anything about it. I don't know anyone who lives there. I don't have a plane ticket. And then there's the movie. My contract. Antonio will expect me on the set Monday morning."

He smiled. "Details," he said softly, and when she parted her lips to tell him that going to Hawaii was impossible, he drew her close and kissed her until she sighed, leaned into his protective embrace and kissed him back.

CHAPTER EIGHT

DETAILS, Falco had said.

That turned out to be an interesting way to describe things.

As soon as they were in the SUV and heading for the freeway, he flipped open his mobile phone and hit a speed dial number. Elle fought back the desire to tell him using a phone while driving was illegal. She had the feeling the man beside her never cared too much about legalities.

The thought should have been worrying.

It was, instead, reassuring. While she was trying to figure out how that could be, she heard him say, "Farinelli? Falco Orsini here."

He was talking with Antonio. Her director. He would not be thrilled to hear Falco didn't want her on the set Monday. An understatement. He would not permit it; she was certain of it. They were on the freeway now and the roar of traffic drowned out Falco's side of the conversation, only the end of it when he said, "Yes, that's correct, I'll be in touch."

Surprised, she looked at him. "Antonio said it would be all right?"

Falco shrugged. "He'll shoot around you."

"Yes, but—"

He reached for her hand and brought it to his mouth.

His lips brushed her fingers. His breath whispered over her skin.

"Stop worrying, okay? I told you, I'll handle everything."

He put her hand back in her lap, flipped his phone open again. She could still feel the electric tingle of his lips on her flesh.

Her heart raced.

She was turning control of her life over to this man. How had that happened? She certainly hadn't given him permission to take charge—but then, she couldn't imagine him ever asking for permission to do anything.

Being with him, putting herself in his hands, was like riding a roller coaster. The nervous anticipation of the long climb to the top, the sharp bite of fear that began at the moment of descent and then the rush, the breathless realization that you'd let go of everything solid and real in favor of the transcendent excitement of just being.

Elle swallowed hard. She didn't like roller coasters. Then, why go on this particular ride? She swung toward Falco, ready to tell him she wouldn't go along with his plans.

"Falco—"

He raised the index finger of the hand that held the phone in acknowledgement.

"Right," he said. "On the ocean. Very private. Limited access. Top-notch security system. Yes, Maui would be perfect. And I'll need a car waiting at the airport. No, I don't care about the make. Just something with lots of horses. And black. Yes, fine. That will do."

Do for whom? No one had made decisions for her in years, especially not a man. Why was she letting such a thing happen now?

"Falco," she said sharply. "We need to discuss this. I've been thinking it over and I'm not at all sure I want to go to Haw—"

But he was already deep in call number three.

"Yes," he said, "that's correct. Immediately. To Hawaii. Just two people."

"Two people?" she blurted.

Falco shut the phone and glanced at her.

"You and me," he said. "Or did you think I'd let you go alone?"

She stared at him. The truth was, she didn't know what to think.

Not anymore.

He drove to LAX, parked at a section new to her and walked her quickly through doors marked ReadyServe Charter Flights.

"We're renting a plane?"

"How long do you think it would take for the world to know Elle Bissette is going to Hawaii if we took a commercial flight?"

"They'll know anyway, once they see my credit card."

"We're using mine."

"But a chartered flight will cost…" She bit her lip. She didn't want to insult him but surely he had to realize that this would run to thousands of dollars. "I mean, my card has no—"

"No dollar limit. But neither does mine."

Did her reaction show on her face? It must have, because he squeezed her hand.

"Trust me," he said quietly. "Can you do that, do you think?"

A better question was, did she have a choice?

There was a counter ahead of them, staffed by a young woman. Falco tugged the ball cap lower on Elle's forehead.

"Keep to the side," he said in a low voice. "Let me do all the talking." Then he let go of her hand, strolled to the counter and flashed a sexy, dazzling smile.

"Hi," he said. "I'm Falco Orsini. I phoned a little while ago."

"Oh, Mr. Orsini. Of course, sir. I have your paperwork all ready."

Elle was all but invisible. The girl hardly glanced in her direction, but then, why would she when Falco was flirting with her?

Not that it mattered.

He was her bodyguard. Their relationship was strictly business. When had she ever wanted any other kind of relationship with a man?

"Never," Elle said under her breath as Falco caught her elbow and began hustling her toward the double doors at the rear of the office.

"Never what?" he said mildly. "Or don't I want to know?" She would have jerked away but his fingers clasped her elbow more tightly. "Just keep moving."

"Don't you want to say goodbye to your little friend?"

Falco chuckled. "Why, honey, I do believe you're jealous."

"You wish."

A sleek silver jet was waiting on the tarmac. Falco walked her toward it.

"When we get to the plane, go up the steps, straight into the cabin."

"Why? Do you expect your fan club to follow you onto the field to say goodbye?"

Falco chuckled. "Nicely done, don't you think?"

"You mean, how you turned her head? Very nicely done, indeed."

"The idea was to keep her eyes from you."

"Yes, well you managed that." Dammit, why did she sound so irritated?

"And without a card from Actor's Equity, either."

She shot him a cold look. His face was expressionless

but amusement danced in his dark eyes. That annoyed her even more.

"Or maybe you'd have preferred it if she'd asked you for your autograph."

Elle narrowed her eyes. "Don't be an ass!"

"An ass." He arched one eyebrow. "Very nice."

"You know what I mean. Of course I didn't want that."

"So, what's the problem?"

The man was infuriating! "There is no problem."

"Yeah, there is." They'd reached the plane. Elle went up the steps, Falco close behind her, and they entered a handsomely appointed cabin. "You're ticked off because I kept that kid from noticing you."

"She wasn't a kid. And there were other ways you could have kept her from noticing me instead of—instead of flirting with her!"

A grin angled across his chiseled mouth. "Ah."

"Ah, what?" Elle folded her arms. "It was wrong, that's all. For all she knew, you and I were—we were—"

"Together," Falco said, a sudden roughness in his voice.

"Yes. No. I only meant—"

He caught her face between his hands and kissed her. Hard. Deep. Kissed her until she moaned into his mouth and wound her arms around his neck. Then, only then, he put her from him.

"I know exactly what you meant," he said, his voice still rough, his eyes hot, his hands slipping to her shoulders. Then he took a long breath and let go of her. "Sit anywhere," he said, as calmly as if nothing had happened. "I'm going to talk to the pilot."

She stared after him, watching that very male walk, that arrogant and, yes, incredibly sexy I-own-the-world swagger. Her heart was beating so hard she could hear it.

What was she doing, going to Hawaii with this man? What

did she know about him, really, beyond the fact that he could talk Antonio Farinelli into changing a shooting schedule, that he was as at ease checking into a cheap motel as he was chartering a flight that had to cost twenty thousand bucks or more?

Was she going from one kind of danger to another?

Logic told her to get off the plane. There was still time.

Falco strolled back into the cabin. "All set," he said. He took a seat and reached for a magazine.

Elle hesitated. Then she sat down as far from him as she could get.

Moments later, they were in the air.

She slept most of the flight, awakening once as Falco draped a light blanket over her.

"Mmm," she whispered, and she must have dreamed that he smiled, leaned down and pressed a kiss to her temple because she surely would not have permitted that to really happen.

She woke to the impersonal touch of his hand on her shoulder.

"We'll be on the ground in twenty minutes," he said briskly. "If you need to use the facilities, now's the time."

Great. Now he was taking charge of her bathroom habits. Elle unsnapped her seat belt, used the lavatory, shuddered at her reflection over the sink. Her hair was lank, her face was pale, she hadn't changed her clothes in, what, almost two days.

As soon as they touched down, she was going to find the nearest mall.

That turned out to be a foolish hope.

The plane landed, taxied to a stop at the terminal. Falco clasped her elbow as if he expected her to bolt and led her to a low, gorgeous shiny black Ferrari. You didn't have to drive one to recognize one, not when you lived in LaLa Land where driving anything that cost less than the national budget of a small nation was evidently against the law.

Falco gave the car a glance, held out his hand so the teenaged kid who'd delivered it could give him the necessary papers to sign. He handed the papers back along with a bill that made the kid's grin spread from ear to ear.

"In," he said brusquely to Elle.

The kid looked at her. Hidden safely behind the ball cap and dark glasses, wanting to stay that way, she had little choice but to obey the command. Still, she couldn't resist clicking her heels and saluting.

"Yessir!"

The kid started to laugh, saw Falco's face and thought better of it.

"All the house stuff—the keys, the gate opener, the paper-work—is in an envelope on the seat."

But Falco had already found the envelope, handed it to Elle and put the car in gear.

Forty minutes later, they pulled up at a massive iron entrance gate.

They had passed no one since leaving the main road. Now, a seemingly endless tangle of grasses and palm trees stretched ahead. If there was really a house here, it was well-hidden.

Elle peered through the windshield. "Are you sure this is it?"

"The GPS says it is." Falco aimed the control device at the gate and depressed the button. There was an audible click and then it swung open.

"Here we go," he said.

The narrow road beyond, bordered by tall native plants, twisted in a series of lefts and right. Whatever lay ahead of them was obscured by the foliage. Then, gradually, the heavy growth cleared, revealing a long shell drive lined with stately palms.

And a house.

Elle caught her breath.

It was an amazing house, all angles and planes standing on a low promontory overlooking a sea so blue it could have been a stage set, except for the white froth of waves breaking against the sand of an equally white beach.

She had spent the flight telling herself whatever Falco had arranged for them here would not matter.

A lie.

This house, this beach, this magic mattered. How could it not? The place was magnificent and secluded and like nothing she had ever seen or imagined.

She must have made some little sound because Falco looked at her as he stopped the Ferrari a few yards from the house.

"Not bad," he said.

Elle swung toward him. "Not bad? It's—"

She saw his face. The big grin. She grinned, too.

"It's not bad," she said, and he laughed, got out of the car and came around to her side, but she was already out of her seat, out of the car and staring at the house. "How did you find it?"

He shrugged and reached for her hand. "I didn't. I called a realtor we've used in the past."

"We?" Elle said carefully.

Falco looked at her. "I'm not involved with anyone."

Her cheeks blazed scarlet. "I didn't mean—"

"Yes," he said, "you did."

He waited for her to deny it. She didn't. She just stared at him, those incredible eyes filled with a variety of emotions. Anger. Embarrassment. And something more, something that made him want to take her in his arms and kiss her.

He closed the distance between them. Said her name. Reached out toward her…

And, as if Fate were the director and this was a movie set, a fat drop of rain hit his head, another hit her nose. In seconds, they'd be caught in a tropical deluge.

They ran for the house.

Just as well, Falco told himself, absolutely just as well. The last thing he needed was to get into this any deeper than he already was.

They went through the house together.

Falco wanted to see how it was set up.

The alarm system was at the top of his list. It was good, maybe very good but he could see ways, low-tech ways, to tweak it. As the realtor had promised, there were absolutely no other houses nearby.

Everything else was fine, too.

The house was built around an atrium. Glass-enclosed. An infinity pool, complete with waterfall. All the rooms opened onto it, and the rooms seemed endless.

Four bedrooms. Six bathrooms. Two half baths. A dining room, a kitchen, a wine storage room, a den, a media room. A living room the size of a basketball court with one entire wall that could be completely opened at the press of a button. A teak terrace wrapped around the part of the house that faced an empty stretch of private, white sand beach. Two miles of beach, according to a cheerful note the realtor had left stuck to the Sub-Zero fridge with a hula dancer magnet.

And, of course, there was the incredibly blue Pacific stretching to the distant horizon.

Elle stood on the terrace and threw her arms wide, as if to encompass all 10,000 or so square feet of the house.

"My God," she said, "it's huge!"

Falco, lounging, arms folded, in the door to the den,

watched her. For a movie star, the lady was surprisingly easy to please.

"Well, yes," he said, "but you never know when you're gonna need some extra space."

She laughed. It was, he thought, a lovely thing to hear.

"When I was growing up, in Beaufort Creek…"

She bit her lip, flashed him a look that could only mean she'd said more than she'd intended.

Falco said, very softly, "Beaufort Creek?"

"Just a place," she said brightly. "Where did you grow up?"

A neat change of subject, but he went with it. "New York. Greenwich Village. Or Little Italy."

She raised her eyebrows. "Which was it?"

"Well, it was Little Italy when my old man bought the first house, maybe even when he bought the second. By the time he'd bought the third, real estate mavens were calling the neighborhood part of the Village."

"I don't understand. You grew up in three different houses?"

Falco grinned. "Three houses, side by side, that he converted into one big house. Believe me, there were times so much construction was going on, we didn't understand it, either."

"We?"

"My brothers and my sisters," he said, and frowned.

How had she managed that? Getting him to talk about himself, especially about his family? He never discussed his family with anyone. Besides, he was the one who was supposed to be getting information from her.

It was just that she was easy to talk to…

"It must be nice," Elle said in a soft voice. "Having brothers and sisters."

"Didn't you?" he said, seeing a way to way to change directions and going for it. "Grow up with brothers and sisters, back in Beaufort Creek?"

She looked at him. "I'm not going to discuss my life with you," she said calmly.

Yes, he thought as she walked back into the house, oh, yes, she would. She was hiding something and she had to tell him what it was. She had to talk to him, and soon.

She had to, if he was going to keep her safe.

The kitchen was clearly a woman's dream.

It was only that he hadn't figured this particular woman was into things like that. But she was, he thought, suppressing a smile as she poked into cabinets and oohed and aahed over the appliances, the dishes, even the flatware.

"Don't tell me you can cook," he said.

She tossed her head. "If you don't want me to tell you I can, then don't ask."

He laughed as he poked into cabinets, too, though his interests were not in dishes but in food. All he came up with was the realtor's idea of a gift basket. A tiny box of crackers. A wedge of cheese. A split of champagne. Two small bottles of Fiji water and a note that said Welcome to Maui.

"Welcome to a tea party for dolls," Falco said glumly. "Okay, we'll head for town. Get some supplies." He made a face. "And clothes. I don't know about you, Bissette, but I'm starting to want to stand upwind of myself."

Elle gave up ogling the Viking range long enough to look at him. "I saw a Walmart on the way here."

He grinned. "You, in a Walmart?"

"There's nothing wrong with Walmart."

"No," he said quickly. Good God, was she actually bristling? She was. There were glints of fire in her eyes. "Absolutely not. Walmarts are, uh, they're great."

"I worked in one."

"Ah. The famous 'what I had to do before I got my first acting break,' huh?"

"I worked in one long before that. And I bought my clothes there, too."

Amazing. A town called Beaufort Creek, and now this. She'd told him more about herself in the past half hour than she had since they'd met…and from what he could remember, there hadn't been a word about Walmart or Beaufort Creek in the studio-scripted story of her life he'd found tucked within the folder his old man had given him.

"Well," he said, with a little smile, "here's your chance to buy some again. How's that sound?"

"Perfect," she said.

Wrong, Falco thought.

The only perfect thing he knew was her.

They drove to town, made a stop at a gas station.

"Pit stop," Falco said, with a quick smile.

There was no need to tell her he'd made a call on the plane while she slept, to a guy who'd served with him and lived here, in the fiftieth state.

"I need a weapon," Falco had said. "Something powerful, not big, easily carried."

The gun was waiting for him there, in bottom of a full wastebasket in the men's room. Falco retrieved it, got behind the wheel of the Ferrari and headed for Walmart.

"It's safer," he said. "It'll probably be more crowded than a regular store and—"

Elle touched a fingertip to his lips. It scalded him. He fought back the desire to suck that sweet finger into his mouth, told himself it was enough that she had touched him without him first touching her, added it to the list of amazing things that had already happened since they'd gotten to Maui.

"Honestly," she said, "I really am fine with Walmart. I can get everything I want here."

She did. Shorts. Tees. Sandals. Jeans. A zippered hoodie for cool evenings. Underwear—white, plain, utilitarian but that didn't keep him from imagining her wearing it and nothing else. Toothpaste, toothbrush, toiletries. Falco dumped similar things into the cart.

They loaded a second cart with groceries. Falco picked up wine, steaks and chops, eggs and bacon, butter and cream and coffee. Elle added vegetables, fruit, whole grain bread and yogurt. She read the labels with the attentiveness of a doctoral student in a chemistry lab.

Amazing, he thought. She didn't just seem comfortable doing this mundane stuff, she seemed to be enjoying it. He knew part of it was probably that they had, at least for the moment, left whomever was stalking her behind. Then again, maybe it was more than that. Maybe it was that she enjoyed being with him...

"All done," Elle said. She smiled at him and that was all it took. He looked into that lovely face, all but hidden by the brim of her cap and the oversized sunglasses, and right there, surrounded by cookies and snacks, he took Elle in his arms and kissed her.

What made it even better was that she sighed and kissed him back.

She was quiet on the drive back to the house.

So was Falco.

Why had he kissed her? He wasn't given to impulsive acts, not in public, especially when they involved women. There'd just been something about the easy way she had of making the best of things, the motel and now the shopping trip. He couldn't imagine any of the women he'd been involved with pushing a cart up and down the aisles of a big box store, picking out plain clothes without complaint.

Ahead, the light turned red. He eased the Ferrari to a stop, glanced idly at the mall across the way. It was small but clearly upscale. That figured, considering the price of real estate once you got along the coast. A Starbucks. A jewelry store. A hair salon.

A place called La Boutique.

There was only one thing in the window. A long gown. Slender straps, supple, softly clinging silk in a color that could only be called topaz.

Or maybe amber. The color of Elle's eyes.

A horn beeped behind them. Falco blinked, put the car in gear, made a sharp turn into the mall and pulled to a stop.

"Forgot to buy coffee," he said briskly.

"But we bought coffee," she said, but he pretended not to hear her and headed for the Starbucks.

He went in. Bought coffee. Mocha Java Bliss, Heavenly Espresso, Capriccio Cappuccino. It didn't matter. He paid for it, then went out the door, gave the Ferrari a quick glance. Elle's face was turned to the road.

Quickly, he slipped inside the boutique.

Five minutes later, he returned to the car and tossed the Starbucks bag into the rear seat. Did Elle notice its bulk? Probably not, because she was silent the rest of the way.

And, once again, so was he.

CHAPTER NINE

OKAY. Maybe he was losing his grip on reality.

First he'd kissed her in a crowded store. An impulsive act he'd quickly regretted. So, how had he made up for it?

Falco's jaw tightened.

By doing something not just impulsive but insane. Why had he bought that gown? Shoes, too. Hey, how could a woman wear a fall of silk the color of autumn leaves with flat leather sandals?

He was out of his mind.

He thought about turning around, going back to the little shop where he'd felt as out of place as snow on a Hawaiian beach, but what would he say to the sales clerk? Sorry but I shouldn't have bought this stuff? The way she'd looked at him, he figured she'd thought he was weird to start with, a man who looked as if he'd slept in his clothes because he had, a two-day stubble on his face…or was it three?

"I want that gown," he'd said, "size six or eight. And shoes to go with it."

The woman hadn't moved until he pulled out his wallet and his black Amex card. That won him a big smile.

"Of course, sir," she'd chirped.

No. Falco blew out a long breath. No, he wasn't going back

there. He'd just hustle the gown and the shoes into the trash and nobody would be the wiser.

Certainly not Elle.

He glanced over at her. The folded arms, the taut profile, eyes straight ahead, chin raised. Thinking about it, it was clear she'd enjoyed the shopping excursion because she'd seen it as a game.

He was, without question, out of his mind.

She wanted this situation to be over with ASAP. And so, absolutely, did he.

What was Falco thinking?

Elle could feel his eyes on her every few minutes but she kept her own focused straight ahead, as if the road that led out of town, then down toward the ocean, required her complete concentration.

Falco knew the way and he was a competent driver. Competent? An understatement. The car was like a growling jungle cat; he handled it with easy self-assurance, one hand on the wheel, one resting lightly on the shift lever.

How could the sight of a man driving a car be sexy?

Elle rolled her eyes.

It wasn't. He wasn't. Not to her, anyway. The word, the very concept, was foreign to her unless she was wearing a designer's creation on a runway or inside character on a film set. Even then, she was pretty much a disaster.

Something was happening. Something was changing. Inside her. Between them. Whatever it was, she didn't understand it, didn't like it, didn't want it…but it was happening just the same.

That kiss. In, of all places, a crowded aisle in a crowded store. Falco's lips moving lightly against hers; hers clinging to his. She'd done nothing to stop it. She hadn't wanted to stop it. He hadn't touched her. No hands. No embrace. Just that hot, sweet, electric fusion of lips until a grumpy female voice said, "Excuse me!" and they'd sprung apart, each of them grabbing a shopping cart, and made for the registers as if their lives depended on it.

It there hadn't been all those people around...

Her throat constricted.

Stress. That's what it was. That, or incipient insanity. There was no other explanation, no reason for that kiss or for her to wonder how it would feel if the house ahead of them—this beautiful, isolated, romantic house Falco had rented—had nothing to do with safety and expediency and had, instead, everything to do with his wanting to be alone with her....

Elle folded her arms.

What on earth was she thinking? She didn't want him wanting that. He was her bodyguard. She was his client. His not altogether willing client, when you came down to it, and that was it.

Why would she ever be stupid enough to want more?

They'd reached the house. She reached for the door handle before he'd brought the car to a complete stop.

"Hey!" He grabbed her arm and jerked her back into her seat. "Didn't anybody ever tell you it's a good idea to wait until a car stops before you get out?"

His tone was curt. It would be. Mr. Orsini didn't like anyone doing something he hadn't given them permission to do. Too bad. She wasn't in the mood to take orders.

Maybe that was the problem.

He'd stormed into her life, uninvited, and taken over. He made decisions without a word or a question, and when had she said he could do that? Never, and that was the point. He had taken over and now she was paying the price for letting him do it. That "woof" she'd barked when he'd told her to stay put today or yesterday or whenever in hell it had been, was no longer a joke. She was behaving like a well-trained dog. Compliant. Obedient. Malleable. And, she was tired of the act.

"Thank you for that helpful information," she said coldly. "I'm sure I'd never have figured it out for myself."

"You have a problem accepting advice?" he said, just as coldly.

"When I need your advice, I'll let you know."

"Do us both a favor, baby, and—"

"That's another thing. I've asked you not to call me that."

His eyes narrowed. From that soft, sweet kiss to this? Never mind that he regretted the kiss. Obviously, so did she. But why? Why should she? That had to be what this was all about, that she'd kissed him in the middle of a store, and whose fault was that? She'd wanted him to kiss her. She'd melted straight into him.

It was time to take a step back. Reassess things. He already knew he'd violated his own rules. What had become of his commitment to keeping things professional? Well, he was returning to that, right now. And she needed to know it.

"Okay," he said briskly, "here's the way things are going to be from now—"

"We need a change in plans."

His eyebrows rose. "Meaning?"

"Meaning, starting now, you're to consult me on decisions."

A cold knot was forming in his gut. "Consult you," he said calmly.

"Yes. You made all these plans—the plane, the house, Hawaii—as if I weren't involved. I don't want that to happen again."

"And I'm to do this because…?"

"Because this is my life!"

"That last I checked, you were standing in a bedroom that had been turned inside-out, wringing your hands and trying to figure out what in hell to do with that life."

She looked as if she wanted to slug him.

"I did not wring my hands. And you didn't give me the chance to figure out anything!"

Falco's lips drew back in a dangerous smile.

"This is all about that kiss."

Elle started to answer. Then she thought better of it and reached again for the door. Falco's hand closed around her wrist.

"You kissed me," he growled. "Now you're behaving as if it was a crime. Would you like to explain that?"

"I kissed you?" She laughed. "Funny, but I don't remember it that way."

"We kissed, okay? So what?"

Pointedly, she looked from him to her wrist.

"Let go of me, Orsini."

"I want an explanation, Bissette. What's this all about?"

What, indeed? She was so angry that she was shaking. He knew damned well what this was all about. He had kissed her. For some reason, she had let it happen. And, yes, she'd let it happen several times and she didn't understand it but she didn't have to.

All that mattered was that it would not happen again.

She knew how these things went.

A man came along, he offered his help, he made you feel safe and then—and then—

Falco's hand tightened on hers. "Answer me, dammit. What's going on?"

Elle raised her chin and looked into his anger-filled eyes.

"What's going on is that you are here solely to protect me."

"You have complaints about how I've been doing that?"

"Yes, I have. You seem to have forgotten your place."

God, where had those horrible words come from? She saw Falco's eyes cloud with rage. She wanted to call back what she'd said, not because she feared him but because it was a lie. She never, ever thought that way about people and she wasn't going to start now, especially with someone like Falco, an honorable, decent man whose only crime was—

Whose only crime was that he had somehow turned her world upside down.

"I've forgotten my place," he said, repeating her words in a low, dangerous voice.

"No," she said quickly, "that isn't what I meant!"

It was too late. He flung her hand from him, opened the door and got out of the car. She scrambled out, too.

"Falco! Please. I didn't mean—"

"Yeah. You did." He swung toward her. She stumbled back. "And you're right. I did forget my place."

"No. I swear, I didn't—"

"Get in the house."

"Falco—"

"I'm going to take a look around."

"What for? We already—"

"It's part of what I have to do to protect you." He reached inside the car, rifled through the bags until he found the one from Starbucks. "You're one hundred percent correct, Ms. Bissette. That's why I'm here."

Elle shook her head. "Listen to me. Please."

"Don't worry about getting the rest of the stuff inside. It's probably within my job description to haul in the groceries, but I'll get your things inside, too, even though some might call that fetching and carrying. But I'll oblige and do it—if you approve, of course. I mean, consider this a consultation."

"You're twisting everything I said!"

"Yes or no? You want me to deal with this stuff or not?"

Shaking with anger, she glared at him over the roof of the Ferrari. "A decent man would accept an apology."

His smile was quick and cold. "But I'm not a decent man. Isn't that pretty much what you just told me?"

"You can go straight to hell!"

"Sounds like a plan," he said, and he turned his back and walked away.

It took her three trips to get the all the things they'd bought into the house, including the groceries, but leaving them for Falco was not an option.

She didn't need anything from him, didn't want anything from him, not even his services as a bodyguard. She'd been doing just fine, handling things on her own.

And she'd handle things on her own, again.

Letting the all-knowing Mr. Orsini into her life had been a mistake, one she'd remedy right away. First thing in the morning, she'd call the airport, call for a taxi, get out of here so fast it would make his head spin. She'd have done it now but she wasn't even sure what time it was.

All she knew was that she needed a bath and a meal and a solid night's rest.

Choosing a bedroom was easy. She took the first one she came to, dumped the bags that held the things she'd purchased on the bed and locked the door behind her.

Falco Orsini was an infuriating, heartless bully. Her temper outburst was his fault. Kissing her, then trying to blame the incident on her...

Elle stalked into the attached marble bathroom, flicked on the light and turned on the hot water tap in the deep soaking tub.

Wait. She'd forgotten something. She hurried into the

bedroom, emptied the contents of her purse on the bed. There it was. The silver frame that held the picture of her and Mama. Tears burned behind her eyes as put her index finger to her lips, then to the picture. She gazed at it for a while. Then she took a deep breath, found the toothbrush and toothpaste she'd bought and returned to the bathroom.

She sniffed at little packets and bottles of oils and bath salts, chose an oil called Tranquility and a matching bar of elegantly wrapped soap. Elle brushed her teeth, stripped off her clothes, made a face and stuffed the clothes into a wicker basket.

The bath was steaming and fragrant. She climbed into the tub, moaned with pleasure and lay back.

Falco Orsini was impossible. He was not a knight in shining armor; he was a man like all other men. That she'd let that slip her mind, even briefly, proved how exhausted she was. The mutilated picture, the note, the mess at the cabin and the condo... All of that had worked against her, had made her vulnerable to letting a man make decisions for her.

And what would you have done if he hadn't made the decisions? If he hadn't followed you to the cabin, or hadn't refused to let you return to your place that night?

Elle gave herself a mental shake. She'd have done what had to be done, that's what. She didn't need the high-and-mighty Mr. Orsini, the police or anyone else. And she'd make that clear tomorrow. Not that Mr. Orsini needed or deserved an explanation. She was taking her life back in her own hands and that was her choice, not his.

She sank lower in the tub. The bath was wonderful. Absolutely wonderful, she thought, closing her eyes as the water lapped against her breasts. Its touch was gentle. Soothing. How would Falco's hands feel against them, instead? His palms cupping their weight. His thumbs moving over her nipples. Lightly. Gently. Then harder as he bent his head to her, pressed his lips to her throat.

Her breasts tingled. A heaviness made its slow way from them to a place low in her belly.

His hands would make their way there, too.

Elle's thighs fell open. The scented water brushed against her flesh. She could feel a pulse beating deep inside her. Beating. Throbbing. Her hand drifted over her belly. Falco's hand would follow that same path and then his mouth. He would stroke her. Part her. Touch her…

She shot upright in the water, heart racing, mind whirling, bile rising in her throat as she shoved the ugly images away. Not just ugly. Horrible. Painful. She knew that, she'd known it forever.

Quickly, she pulled the drain plug and traded the tub for the shower stall, where she scrubbed her skin until it was reddened, washed her hair and made quick work of it.

To hell with the shampoo and conditioner she'd bought. All she wanted now was to get dressed.

The clothes she'd bought lay on the bed. The clothes Falco had bought. He'd used his credit card as if the shopping trip was his to control.

Control was what he was all about. What men were all about. Whatever security company he worked for would, she knew, pick up the tab, but to hell with that. Before she left tomorrow, she'd write him a check for the chartered flight, the house, the shopping trip…

How could an hour in a faceless store have been so much fun?

"What kind of cereal do you like?" she'd said, and he'd answered by plucking a box of sugar-sweetened junk from the shelf. "Yuck," she'd said, grabbing it and putting it back, laughing at the way he'd groaned when she added a box of unsweetened granola to the cart instead, laughing just before he'd kissed her, before he'd made her heart almost stop with that sweet, sweet kiss….

"Stop it," Elle said firmly.

Hell. She'd forgotten to buy pj's. No matter. She dressed quickly: underwear, T-shirt, white jeans, everything clean and fresh against her skin. She'd caught Falco biting back a smile at her choice of underthings. It had made her blush. Would he smile if he saw her wearing them? Not that he ever would but…

Her breath caught. "Stop it," she said again, her voice sharp and a little raw.

Her thoughts were wandering across a wild landscape that had nothing to do with reality. She was tired, was the problem.

And hungry.

Her belly gave a monumental growl.

Breakfast seemed a lifetime ago. There was lots of food in the kitchen. They'd bought cheese and ham, and peanut butter and jelly because Falco had said—with a straight face—that PB and J on white bread was a staple of life.

Elle eased the door open.

The house was silent. Falco's plans had probably mirrored hers. A hot shower, then a nap. She could picture him now, that long, leanly muscled body sprawled naked across the bed.

A frisson of heat shimmered through her body.

Enough. She needed a meal and then some sleep. No. Not a meal. A sandwich would be quicker. She could be out of the kitchen before Falco so much as stirred.

She moved down the hall quickly, silent on bare feet. The kitchen was just a couple of feet away….

Damn, damn, damn!

Falco had beaten her to it. Shirtless, barefoot, wearing only jeans, his dark hair damp and glittering with drops of water, he stood with his back to her at a long granite counter. The loaf of white bread was beside him, the opened jars of peanut butter and jelly next to it. From his motions, she figured he was making a sandwich.

She watched, transfixed, as the muscles in his shoulders and triceps flexed. Her eyes swept downward. He had a powerful-looking back, a narrow waist. His jeans were low on his hips. Was the top button undone? Was that why they hung that way?

And what did it matter?

Why this sudden dryness in her mouth? The equally sudden leap of her heart? Elle took a quick step back.

"Want one?" he said casually.

Falco had sensed her presence and asked the question without turning around. A peace offering? Well, why not. They had hours to get through before she could leave, Elle reminded herself, and she moistened her lips with the tip of her tongue.

"I, ah, I… Yes, thanks. I'd love a sandwich."

He motioned toward one of the counter stools to his left. She shook her head, even though she knew he couldn't see her.

"There must be something I can do to help."

"You can pour us some milk. I'm not usually a milk kind of guy but when it comes to PB and J…"

"The drink of choice. I know."

Elle searched for tall glasses, found them, poured the milk. She put the glasses on the counter, added napkins and silverware and plates.

There was nothing left to do except sit down and watch him put the finishing touches on the sandwiches.

"Kind of like being at one of those sushi restaurants," he said. "You know, where you sit at the counter and get to watch guys wielding knives like homicidal jugglers."

She laughed. "I'm always surprised they end their shifts with five fingers still on each hand."

Falco turned toward her, reaching for the plates. The breath caught in her throat. She'd guessed right. Yes, button at the waistband of his jeans was undone. And, yes, the faded denim hung precariously low on his hips. And yes, oh, yes, he was a magnificent sight, all those sculpted muscles in his shoulders and arms, the cut abs, the dark whorl of hair on his chest that arrowed down and disappeared under the waistband of the jeans…

"What I think," he said, "is that I owe you an apology."

Elle's gaze flew to his. "It was my fault," she said quickly. "I don't know what made me say such an awful thing."

He nodded, his eyes on hers.

"We were both quick on the trigger. And some of what you said was right. I have made a lot of decisions without checking with you first. I shouldn't have done that."

"You made necessary decisions. I know that. It's just that—"

"You're accustomed to making your own decisions."

"Yes."

"Sure. I understand." He hesitated. "And about that kiss…"

She felt her face heat. "Really, there's no need to—"

"I was the one who initiated it. I've initiated every move I've made on you, baby, but they weren't 'moves,' not the way you think. I…hell, I never get involved with the people I'm helping, never step over the boundaries." He snorted and ran a hand through his hair. "There I go again. Calling you 'baby' when you've specifically asked me—"

"Don't stop."

His eyes met hers. "What?"

"I said—I said, don't stop calling me 'baby.'" By now, she knew her face was blazing. "I—I like it. The way you say it. As if—as if it means something to you."

His eyes turned black. "You mean something to me," he said in a low voice.

"You don't have to say—"

He came toward her, put a finger gently over her still-parted lips. His skin was warm; all she had to do was ease the very tip of her tongue between her lips and she could taste him.

"That's one of my flaws," he said. "I tend to say the things I mean. And I mean that, Elle. You—you've become important to me."

She sighed. Her breath was warm against his finger. A shudder went through him as he slid his hand into her hair.

"I want to kiss you," he said roughly. "Hell, I'm going to kiss you. And if that isn't what you want—"

Elle made a little sound, leaned forward and brought her mouth to Falco's. He didn't move, not for a long minute. Then he groaned, wrapped his arms around her and lifted her from the stool. Her arms went around his neck; her legs closed around his hips and he kissed her again, the kiss deepening and deepening until she was moaning into his mouth.

"Elle." He leaned his forehead against hers. "Honey, I want to make love with you."

"I know."

He gave a gruff laugh. Of course, she knew. His erection was enormous and her pelvis was pressed hard against it.

"Tell me it's what you want, too."

He could feel her heart, racing like a tiny bird's against his. She was trembling, breathing fast. He drew her even closer.

"Baby. What is it? Are you afraid of me?"

"No," she said quickly. "Never of you."

"What, then? The—" He hesitated. "The 'sex thing'? Have you had a bad experience? Because if you have—"

"It's—it's something like that."

Who had done this to her? How? What had some bastard done to this beautiful, intelligent, amazing woman? His arms tightened around her.

"I've never—I've never wanted to be with a man before. I can hardly believe it's what I want now. At least—at least, I think it's what I want. But if it's not… I wouldn't want to disappoint you."

"You could never disappoint me," he said fiercely. "If it's not what you want, we'll stop." And I'll die, he thought, but he'd do that rather than do anything to hurt this woman.

She gave a watery laugh. "Men don't stop."

Falco fought to control his fury.

"I am me, honey. Falco Orsini. I am not 'men.' I'd never do anything to hurt you, Elle. I swear it, with all my heart."

She drew back a little and looked at him.

"Just what a guy wants, I'm sure," she said, with a sad attempt at a smile. "To talk a moment like this straight into the ground."

"What this guy wants is to hold you. To kiss you. To sleep with you in my arms. And maybe that's all we should even consider tonight." He gave a little laugh. "Assuming it is night," he said. "I seem to have lost track of time."

Elle stared at him. "Do you think you could really do that?"

What he thought was that by morning he might be dead from the aching need to make love to her, but if being held in his arms was all she wanted, that was all that would happen.

"Remember what you said," she told him solemnly, "about only saying what you really mean."

Falco sighed. "I want to make love to you, baby. To change whatever it is you think you know about sex. If that's not what you want, I'll just hold you while we sleep." He paused. "Or you can trust what I said. About making love and stopping if you want to stop." He smiled. "Your decision to make, Ms. Bissette."

A day ago, an hour ago, she might have said no man could manage sleeping with a woman without sex, but if Falco said he could do it, she believed him. If he said he could stop—stop doing the things men did if she asked him to stop doing them—she believed that, too.

So—so maybe she could let him kiss her. Caress her. And he'd stop when she told him to stop. Because she would tell him to stop. Absolutely, she would.

"Elle?" He cleared his throat. "There's a third option, honey. I'll let go of you, we go to our separate rooms—"

Elle leaned forward and stopped his words with a kiss.

"Take me to bed, Falco," she whispered. "Please. Take me to bed and make love to me."

CHAPTER TEN

ELLE'S WHISPERED words raced through Falco's blood like a fast-moving drug.

If someone had asked, he'd have said he knew all the sexy things a woman could whisper to a man.

Wrong.

Elle's simple words were the most erotic he'd ever heard.

His answer was in his kiss as he carried her through the silent house, not to the bedroom he'd chosen only because it had been the nearest at hand, but past it, to the master suite. Its walls were almost entirely glass, open on one side to the sea and on the other to the cascade of water that tumbled into the atrium pool.

The bed, a four-poster, hung in sheer white lace, dominated the room.

He imagined taking her to it, laying her on it, baring her to his eyes, his hands, his mouth.

But he didn't.

Elle's lips trembled beneath his. Her heart raced against his palm. She wanted him but she was frightened.

Falco was determined to replace that fear with joy even if it took every bit of self-control he possessed.

He kissed her again. Then, slowly, he put her on her feet.

She made a little sound when her breasts brushed his bare chest, caught her breath when the heavy thrust of his erection pressed against her belly. When she would have stepped back, he gathered her in his arms, kept her close.

"That's just my body telling yours how much I want you." His voice was low and rough but the hand he put under her chin was gentle. "Don't be afraid, baby. I won't hurt you. I promise."

He kissed her, soft kisses that belied the hunger inside him until finally he felt her lips soften and cling to his. He took the kiss deeper little by little, touching the tip of his tongue to the tender inside flesh of her bottom lip. He knew he had to go slowly, that everything that came next hinged on it.

And he could do it.

He was a man who had built his life on self-discipline.

Surely, he could carry that ability into this. Into holding back. Into being content just to taste her. Into keeping from cupping her face, parting her lips with his, plunging deep, deep into the honeyed sweetness of her mouth…

Falco groaned.

Elle tensed. "What?" A quick, uneasy breath; she put her hands on his chest. "Am I doing this wrong?"

His throat constricted. He wanted to groan again. Or maybe curse, not at the woman in his arms but at whatever—whomever—had left her feeling this way. Instead, he forced a quick smile.

"No, honey. No, you're doing it just right. It's just that you taste so good…." The hell with it. He could cup her face, lift it to his, kiss her gently. Like that. Exactly like that. Again and again and suddenly she was on her toes, her hands locked around his neck, her lips open to his.

"Yes," he whispered, "yes, that's the way."

"Falco," she said, just that, and he gathered her against him, kissed her mouth, her throat, and she was trembling again but he knew it wasn't with fear, it was with what was happening, what she felt, what he was making her feel, and then he stopped thinking, stopped planning, and his kisses deepened, his hands moved over her, stroking, cupping, caressing until she was making soft little cries and clinging to him as if he was all that could keep her from falling.

He slid his hand under her T-shirt. Up her back, along the sweet, silken warmth of her skin. His palm spread over the side of her breast. She caught her breath and he waited, waited…

His thumb brushed over her nipple.

She sighed against his mouth.

He stroked her again. Felt the nub of flesh harden, felt it press against his thumb. Another sigh. A moan. Falco moved his hand, cupped her breast, bit back a groan at the delicate weight of it in his hand.

She moved.

Moved against him.

Her hips. Her thighs.

A shudder went through him.

He drew back. Put an inch of space between them but it wasn't enough, how could it be when it felt as if an entire room wouldn't be enough to keep his erection from pressing into her belly? He was harder than he'd ever been in his life, so hard that he hurt…and she wasn't leaving space between them anyway, she was moving closer, clasping his shoulders, raising herself to him.

On a low growl, Falco caught Elle's elbows and put her from him. She swayed, blinked her eyes open and stared up at him.

"Falco?"

He dragged air into his lungs.

"I can't," he said. "Honey, I'm sorry. I thought I could do this. I really thought…" Another harsh breath. "But I can't."

Tears rose in her eyes. "Yes. I mean—I mean, no. Why should you?" Elle stepped back, wrapped her arms around herself. "Of course, you can't. I shouldn't have asked—"

"Dammit!" He grabbed hold of her shoulders, lifted her to her toes. "What I'm trying to tell you is that I can't go slow and easy. I want too much. Do you understand?"

Elle swallowed hard. "You want to—to go to bed. Straight to bed. I should have—"

"Hell, no. I don't want to drag you into bed. I want to touch you first. See you. And you're not ready for that."

"See me, how?" Her eyes flew to his. "You mean, un-dressed?"

Her voice was low. In any other set of circumstances, her answer, the look she gave him, might have made him laugh, but laughter was the last thing in his mind at that moment. Instead, her expression, the response…both filled him with an awful combination of anger and sorrow.

"Undressed," he said gruffly. "Yes."

She nodded. He could almost see her processing his words. Then she crossed her arms, grasped the hem of her T-shirt. Falco caught her wrists, brought her hands to his lips and kissed them.

"No. I don't want you to do anything just for me, baby. That's not what making love is all about."

"I want you to see me," she whispered.

"Are you sure?" She nodded. "Then," he said, "then, let me do that."

Her hands fell to her sides. Falco reached for the hem of her T-shirt, drew it over her head and tossed it aside. God, she was beautiful. Honeyed skin. Demure white cotton bra. He'd watched her buy it, watched her bypass lace and satin for this. It had made him smile.

Now, it made his body tighten with hunger.

He waited, mentally counted to ten before he spoke again. "I'm going to take your jeans off, too." His voice was rough as sandpaper. He cleared his throat. "Is that okay, Elle?"

"Yes," she whispered, her face bright with color.

His hands felt huge and clumsy as he reached for the button, then the zipper of her jeans. The hiss of the metal teeth parting seemed inordinately loud, but then, maybe not.

Maybe it wasn't half as loud as the hammering beat of his heart.

Slowly, he slid the jeans down her hips. Her legs. He wanted to squat down, lift her foot, ease the jeans all the way off, but he didn't trust himself, he knew the temptation to put his face against her belly might be more than he could handle. He let the jeans slither to the bamboo floor, took her hands, held them to steady her as she stepped free of them.

Then he looked at her.

Long, dark hair, falling over her shoulders. A face free of makeup. The plainest possible bra and panties. And a beauty so pure it stole his breath away.

Falco's heart kicked against his ribs as he drew her into his arms and kissed her. Lightly. Gently. Told himself to keep it that way but she moved closer to him, framed his face with her hands. Opened her mouth to his and he slid his hands behind her. He hadn't had trouble opening a bra since high school, but now his fingers felt huge and clumsy and, it seemed forever but, thank you, God, at last, the bra opened.

Elle's reaction was to clasp it to her.

Falco's hands closed over hers.

"I want to see you, baby," he said thickly.

A heartbeat's hesitation. Then she let go of the white cotton and it drifted to the floor. His eyes held hers. Then, slowly, he let them fall to her breasts. Ah, they were perfect. Small. Round. Nipples a pale, seashell pink. He raised his eyes to her face, watched her as he traced the outline of one perfect nipple with the tip of his index finger.

"Do you like that?" he whispered.

She moaned. It was all the answer he needed. His hands went to the waistband of the innocent white cotton panties; slowly, he eased them down her long legs. He bent, steadied her as she stepped free of them, fought back the desire to kiss his way up those long legs and bury his face in the soft, dark curls between her thighs and, instead, stood up straight and reached for her again.

Elle shook her head.

"I want…" Her tongue swiped across her bottom lip. "I want…" The rest was an inaudible whisper.

"Honey. I don't know what you said. I couldn't hear—"

"I said—I said, I want to see you, too."

He swallowed. "What?"

"I want to see you naked. That's all. Just to see you."

Sweat beaded on his forehead. He was never going to survive this. Why had he thought he could?

"Falco? Could I—could I see you? Please?"

His hands fumbled at the zipper of his jeans. He took a breath, got it open, pushed the jeans down. He had not put on underwear after he'd showered and now his swollen penis sprang free. His sense of relief was profound.

Profound, but short-lived because—

Because, she was looking at his aroused flesh. Just looking, not touching, and if this kept up, he was going to disgrace himself.

Where was his self-control? That control he prided himself on, that control that always, always kept him in charge of what happened, in bed and out.

"Dammit," he growled, and when she looked up at him he thought, the hell with this and he gathered her into his arms and kissed her, kissed her hard, one hand in her hair, the other holding her tightly against him. He'd do this, kiss her, feel her, let her feel him and then he'd tell her he'd been crazy to think he could pull this off, that he was too old to play doctor.

But how could he do any of those things when Elle was rising on her toes, winding her arms around his neck, meeting his kisses with kisses of her own?

"Please," she sobbed against his lips, "Falco, please, please, please…"

His heart thundered.

Whispering her name, he scooped her up, carried her to the bed. Tumbled onto it with her. Kissed her mouth, her throat, her breasts, exulting in her cries, her sobs.

And tried, one final time, to hang on to sanity.

"Elle…"

There was warning in his voice. She heard it but instead of frightening her, it filled her with ecstasy. She wanted this, wanted him, wanted everything he was, everything he had to give.

"Falco," she said softly, and she touched him. Danced her fingers the length of his rigid flesh, closed as much of her hand around him as she could, felt the throb of life within that part of him that was all male.

"Elle!" The breath hissed from his lips. He took her hand, brought it to her side. "Elle…I'm not a saint…"

She reached up. Kissed his mouth. Kissed him long and deep and sweetly until he groaned and parted her thighs.

She sobbed as he entered her. Slowly. God, so slowly.

Her head fell back against the pillows. She was coming apart. Coming undone. She was flying, blazing across the sky like a shooting star.

"Falco," she sobbed and he said her name, threw back his head and flew into the heavens with her.

* * *

She awoke hours later.

At least, it felt like hours later. Time had lost all meaning. Perhaps they'd slept the day away. Or the night. Whichever it was, Elle came awake draped over Falco like a blanket, her face buried against his throat, his arms holding her close.

It should have been uncomfortable. He was hard, muscled, lean. And his embrace made it almost difficult to breathe.

But it wasn't uncomfortable. It was wonderful. Her lips curved in a smile. She had never felt this happy, this safe. It was as if she belonged here, with this man, as if she'd been created for this.

Her smile faded.

What was she thinking? This, being here, being with Falco…it was all a fantasy. It was worse than that. Falco had only come into her life because the past was finally catching up to her.

If he knew that past, if anyone knew it…

"Hey."

He was awake. She shut her eyes, opened them again, lifted her head and forced a smile.

"Hey, yourself," she said, and her heart turned over. He was so beautiful! She knew he'd groan if she told him that but it was true, he was beautiful. His dark hair was mussed, he had even more of that five o'clock shadow she'd always thought made a man look grungy but made him look almost unbearably sexy. There were laugh lines at the edges of his eyes and a tiny little white line she'd never noticed until now….

"It's a scar," he said softly.

"Was I staring?" She blushed. "Sorry. I didn't mean to—"

"No, it's cool." He smiled. "I like it when you stare at me." His hand slid into her hair; he brought her face to his and kissed her. "Are you all right, baby?"

"Yes." She could feel her color deepening. "I mean—"

"I know what you mean. And I'm happy to hear it."

His words were spoken in a tender whisper. "Tender" was something she couldn't afford. She couldn't let him get too close. For her sake—

And, she thought with a shudder, for his. How come that hadn't occurred to her before?

She took a breath, drew back as far as his encircling arms permitted and flashed a bright smile.

"Yes," she said, "and thank you for that."

His eyes narrowed. "For what?"

"For, you know, for helping me, ah, for helping me get past my, ah, my problem."

She squealed as he rolled her onto her back. He lay above her, his body pinning hers to the mattress, his hands wrapped around her wrists, cold fire in his eyes.

"Thank you?" he said in an ominous whisper.

"Yes. You know. For—"

"Maybe you're going to recommend me to your friends."

"No!" Her breath caught. "I didn't mean that as an insult, I only meant—"

His mouth swooped down and captured hers, his kiss hard and merciless until, despite her best intentions, she moaned his name in a way that made him let go of her hands. His arms went around her; she wrapped hers around him and the kiss changed, became soft and yes, tender, so tender that she wanted to weep.

"I'm sorry," she whispered. "Falco, I'm so sorry. What happened just now—"

"You and me," he said gruffly, "making love."

"Yes. It was—it was—"

"Yeah." A cheeky grin tweaked the corners of his mouth. "It damned well was."

Elle snorted. "Did anyone ever tell you that you have an oversized ego?"

He moved against her. "I'm just an oversized guy."

She didn't want to laugh but she couldn't help it. He was impossible. She told him so.

"You are impossible," she said, trying for stern and not even coming close.

Falco smiled. He kissed her. Kissed her again. Soft, teasing kisses that lengthened and deepened until her bones had absolutely melted.

"So is this," he whispered, "impossibly wonderful." And then he was inside her again, moving inside her, taking her up and up and up and within seconds, nothing else mattered but him.

She wouldn't shower with him.

She wouldn't even leave the bed as long as he was still in the room.

She knew it was foolish, that he knew her body with shocking intimacy, but that didn't mean—it didn't mean she could walk around in front of him without clothes on.

He didn't argue, not once he saw that she meant it. Instead, he kissed the tip of her nose, rose from the bed and strolled toward the adjoining marble bathroom. She tried to avert her eyes. Yes, they'd been intimate, but seeing him, seeing him naked, that part of him naked…

"I would never hurt you, Elle," he said softly.

She looked up. He was standing in the bathroom doorway, not just unashamedly naked but unashamedly beautiful.

Tears rose in her eyes.

She blinked them back, took a deep breath, tossed back the duvet and went to him. He gathered her against him.

"What happened to you?" her knight in shining armor said, so ferociously that it almost broke her heart.

She shook her head, burrowed closer. After a very long time, he brushed his lips lightly over hers.

"Okay," he said, as if nothing had happened, "shower time."

The peanut butter and jelly sandwiches he'd made hours ago were still on the counter.

Elle touched one with a fingertip and winced. "Hard as stone." She looked up and smiled. "I don't think the *P* in PB and J is supposed to stand for 'petrified.' They must have sat here for hours...."

She realized what she'd said and blushed. Lord, he loved the way she blushed, Falco thought as he drew her into his arms.

"Hours," he said softly. "But not half long enough."

He kissed her. Sweet kisses that grew deeper. Quick kisses that grew longer. Kisses that made their breathing quicken until he groaned and leaned his forehead against hers.

"If we don't eat something soon," he said huskily, "the realtor's going to come by one morning and find us as petrified as those sandwiches."

Elle laughed and gave him a gentle push. "I'll cook something. What would you like?"

"Hey, you think I've waited for peanut butter and jelly all this time only to give up on them now? Let's go, woman. Same as before. You pour the milk, I'll make the sandwiches."

They worked side by side and wolfed down their meal while sitting on stools at the granite kitchen counter. Four for Falco, two for her.

"The wardrobe mistress will kill me," Elle said mournfully.

He grinned. "That's how I got this scar," he said, touching his finger to the little white line she'd noticed earlier. "Defending myself against a PB and J attack."

Elle raised her eyebrows.

"My brother, Nick. We were maybe four and five, something like that. He made himself a sandwich. I stole half of it and he came after me. We'd been playing *Star Wars*, you know, the lightsaber thing? Anyway, Nick swung, got lucky and got me. I retaliated, of course—"

"Of course," Elle said. She didn't really accept the story. She suspected the truth was something much darker, but she smiled, picturing him as a little boy.

"And we both went down in a heap. Well, Rafe had left a Tonka Payloader on the floor and—"

"You have two brothers?"

"Three. Nicolo. Raffaele. And Dante." Falco ate the last bite of his sandwich. "And two sisters. Anna and Isabella."

"Oh, that's nice. To have such a big family, I mean."

Falco laughed. "It's nice most of the time. Sometimes, it's a pain in the, ah, in the butt. How about you?"

Elle's smile faded. "How about me, what?"

"Do you have sisters? Brothers?"

"No."

"No, what?"

"No," she said, "there's just me."

Her tone had become cool. Falco cocked his head. "And?"

"And, what?" Elle slid off the stool and put her plate in the sink.

"And, why is talking about family such a big deal?"

"It isn't," she said, even more coolly.

"Trust me, honey. It isn't always my favorite topic, either. I mean, Izzy and Anna, Nick and Rafe and Dante… They're great. So is my mom. But anybody mentions my old man—"

"Don't tell me," Elle said, her voice not cool but frigid. "You and your father have—what's the current term? You have 'issues.' What, he didn't let you borrow the family car when you were seventeen?"

Falco narrowed his eyes. "My father's a thug," he said carefully. "His name is Cesare Orsini. Maybe you haven't heard of him, but, trust me, the cops sure have."

"Oh." Elle reached out her hand. "Falco. I didn't mean—"

"I know you didn't, baby. So, whatever it is about your family that upsets you—"

She laughed. At least, he thought it was a laugh. But it wasn't. She was weeping.

"Ah, honey, I'm an idiot. Come here. Let me hold you."

She shook her head and pushed past him. He thought about stopping her but he didn't. Instead, he watched her go through the atrium doors and on into the starlit night, watched as she padded barefoot through the sand, to the beach. Then he went after her. They were as safe here as he'd been able to make it: the gates, the alarm system, the little touches he'd added of his own, but no way would he let her out of his sight until he got the son of a bitch who was stalking her.

A chill danced down Falco's spine.

He knew a lot of people who had what Elle had called "issues" with their families. It was, more or less, a sign of the times. Hell, he had his own thing about his father. So did his brothers.

But Elle's reaction just now...

His steps quickened.

He had held off asking her what she knew about her stalker though he suspected she knew something. He hadn't pushed her on why she didn't want the cops involved, either; she was a celebrity and maybe she just didn't want that kind of press. He hadn't pressured her because she'd been through a lot in the past few days. He'd figured on giving her a little time before asking more questions.

Some seventh sense, some instinct told him that the time for asking them was now.

He caught up to her at the surf line, fell in beside her as she walked. She shot him a poisonous look but he ignored it.

"What's going on?"

"I don't know what you're talking about."

"Elle," he said firmly. He caught her elbow, turned her toward him. "You have to tell me. You know you do."

"Go back to the mainland, Falco. Just—just leave me alone."

"The hell I will! I can't protect you without knowing what you know about this maniac."

Her eyes flashed. "Is that what you call taking me to bed? Was that about protecting me?"

She was deliberately trying to make him angry. He knew it, but that didn't make it any easier.

"Answer the question. Tell me what you know."

"What I know is that that we had sex."

He wanted to shake her. Or kiss her. Instead, he grabbed her by the shoulders and hauled her to her toes.

"Dammit, woman! We made love."

"It was sex," she said bitterly. "And I should have known you'd think that grants you some kind of ownership—"

Falco cursed, pulled her against him and captured her lips with his. She struggled, tried to twist free—and then she sobbed his name, wound her arms around him and kissed him back with all the hunger in her heart. He swept her into his arms, carried her to the house and to bed. They made love again and again, until she wept with joy. One last kiss and then she fell asleep in his arms.

Falco remained awake, eyes fixed on the ceiling.

He had violated the principles by which he lived, giving in to his emotions, letting them take him deep into uncharted waters—but he didn't care. If he had to, he would give his life for the woman beside him.

He had only known her a few short days but she had come to mean more to him than he'd ever imagined possible.... And more than he wanted to define.

CHAPTER ELEVEN

HE ASKED no more questions.

His time with Special Forces had taught him the importance of knowing as much about the enemy as he could. Later, doing clandestine work for private clients, he'd adhered to that rule. The Turkish couple he'd recently helped had accused him of indifference because he'd demanded they bare their souls to him, but what he'd ultimately learned had been instrumental in helping him find, and save, their son.

The bottom line was that the one stipulation he always required was full access to information. A client either gave it up freely or Falco would go after it.

This was different. There wasn't a way in hell he'd do that to Elle.

It made his job more difficult but he cared too much about her to force her to divulge whatever dark secrets she possessed. And he cared more and more about her as the days, and the nights, slipped by.

Time had become as fluid as the ocean. There was no beginning, no end. There were only long, sweet days and long, hot nights. The hours blurred into each other, every one of them filled with pleasure.

Not that they did anything special.

Long walks on the beach, with Elle plucking what Falco would have sworn was every shell they saw from the sand. Lazy hours by the pool. They played poker after Falco taught her the game, betting with the shells she'd collected, then with play money filched from a Monopoly set they found on a shelf in the den.

He let her win most of the hands and then, to make it interesting, he said, he suggested betting with the clothes they were wearing.

Surprisingly enough, he began winning.

"You lost all those other times on purpose," she said with mock indignation when she'd been reduced to only an oversized white T-shirt and her panties.

"Hey," he said, eyes filled with innocence, "are you calling me a liar?"

"I'm calling you a cheat, Orsini," she said, squealing as he tossed his cards aside and grabbed her.

They laughed and tussled, and gradually the laughter became sighs and the tussles became touches, and they forgot all about poker and made love until Falco thought his heart would burst with happiness.

Because, God, he was happy. Not that he hadn't been happy before but never like this, doing such mundane things. He was not a man who enjoyed mundane things, at least, he never had before. He lived for risk, for danger, for walking on the edge. And there was nothing risky about those long walks or lying in the sun or driving to the little farm stand they'd discovered, buying fresh mahi mahi and grouper, dew-covered fruits and vegetables.

He'd found condoms there, too, and he bought an amount he figured would have made Elle blush if she knew, but the simple truth was, he wanted to make love with her all the time and to his joy, she wanted the same thing.

And then, one night as he grilled their meal in the atrium and Elle emerged from the house with the salad he looked at her and he thought maybe there was something a little dangerous about this, about what he felt when he looked at her....

Something must have shown on his face.

"What?" Elle said.

"I, ah, I was just thinking that, uh, that my brothers would be proud if they could see me now."

Smiling, she poured two glasses of chilled Prosecco and handed him one.

"Because?"

"Because I've turned into a world-class chef." He grinned at the look on her face, cut off a tiny bit of the grilled fish with a fork and held it out. "Taste this and tell me it isn't the best grilled mahi mahi you've ever eaten."

She leaned forward. Parted her lips. Falco moved fast, pulled back the fork and put his mouth against hers.

Elle sighed. "Delicious," she said softly.

He kissed her again, then popped the bite of fish into her mouth.

"Mmm. That's delicious, too."

"What did I tell you? Falco Orsini, master chef. Don't laugh. Compared to the last fish-type dish I cooked, this is fancy stuff."

"'Fish-type dish,' huh?" Elle smiled as she propped her hip against the table. "I'm almost afraid to ask."

"Oh, ye of little faith." Falco slid a spatula under the fish and flipped it onto a platter. "Tuna."

"Ahi tuna?"

His lips twitched. "Bumble Bee. Chicken of the Sea. I'm not particular about the brand."

"You mean, canned tuna?"

"Toss in some penne pasta, cream of mushroom soup..."

"Yuck."

"Okay, then." He drew out a chair for her. She sat down, and he sat opposite. "The tuna, parmesan cheese, frozen peas—"

"Double yuck." She paused. "You want a gourmet meal, it's macaroni and cheese."

He laughed.

"Go on, Orsini, laugh. But until you've cooked up a box of mac and cheese, maybe add some diced ham if you want to be fancy…" She laughed, too. "No, huh?"

Falco spread his napkin in his lap. "My mother already figures I have the eating habits of a barbarian."

"Is she a good cook?"

"Is she a…" He rolled his eyes. "She's Sicilian. Of course, she's a good cook. Well, she is just as long as you don't balk at what she thinks you like to eat."

"Thinks you like to eat?"

"Yeah. She's got these ideas. For instance, my sister, Izzy, went on this vegan kick one time and Mama said no problem, she'd cook vegan."

"But?"

"But, she thought 'vegan' meant adding vegetables to things. There was no convincing her that chicken and pork and steak, vegetables tossed in or not, wasn't 'vegan.'"

Elle forked up some salad. "Uh-oh."

"Uh-oh, is right. It was interesting."

"I'll bet."

"And then there's Dante, who can't stand the sight of pesto. Somehow, Mama got the idea he loves it." He chuckled. "You cannot imagine all the ways she's come up with to serve my poor brother what she's sure is his favorite dish."

Elle's smile was soft and wistful. "It must be nice, having a big family."

They'd had this conversation before. It hadn't gone well.

Falco figured it was worth another try. He knew, in his gut, whatever Elle wasn't willing to talk about was somehow connected to the topic of family.

"So," he said casually, "you didn't, huh?"

She shook her head. "No."

"Just, what, you and your mom and dad?"

"My dad died when I was little."

"Ah. Just you and your mom, then."

There was a slight pause. Then Elle shrugged. "Yes."

"She never remarried?"

Another pause. "She did, after a while."

Her voice was suddenly tight. Falco felt a tingling on the nape of his neck.

"Nice. That she met somebody, I mean, and fell in love."

"Very nice," Elle said in a flat voice.

"It wasn't?"

"He said he'd take care of us. See, we were dirt poor."

That surprised him. "But your bio—"

She looked up. "You've read that nonsense?"

"On the plane flying out to L.A. It said—"

"I know what it said. That I grew up in San Francisco. That I had private tutors."

"Not true, huh?"

She shook her head, kept her eyes on her plate as if it were the most interesting thing she'd ever seen. "I grew up poor."

"In a place called Beaufort Creek."

She looked up. "Yes. That's where I was born. But I lived in different places after that before I finally moved to New York."

"Moved to New York, and started modeling."

"And started modeling," she said, her tone flat again. "You have a problem with…" She sighed. "Sorry."

"No," he said quickly, reached for her hand and held it

tightly in his. "I'm the one who's sorry. I guess I seemed a little, you know, a little hinky about the lingerie stuff."

The breath sighed from her lungs. "I didn't want to sign that contract. But I knew it was a big chance, that it could lead to bigger and better work—"

"Elle." Falco put down his fork. "Honey, you don't owe me or anybody else an explanation."

"If I'd never posed for that last damned picture, he might never have found—"

She fell silent. Falco's hand tightened on hers.

"Who?" he said softly. "Who is he?"

"I only meant—you know, I meant 'he' as in—as in the man stalking me."

She was lying. Her eyes were dark with despair. Her mouth was trembling. Now, when she was so vulnerable, was the time to pursue the topic. She'd break in five minutes....

Instead, Falco shot from his seat, went to her and wrapped her in his arms.

"I can't," she whispered. "Please, please, don't ask me to talk about it...."

"Hush," he said, and he tilted her face to his, kissed her until the darkness in her eyes faded and despair died in the flame of passion.

They went for a drive a couple of days later. On the way home, Falco pulled in to the big mall where they'd bought food and clothes, and stopped outside a FedEx store.

"FedEx?" Elle said, puzzled.

"Man does not live by mahi mahi alone."

She laughed. "Seriously, Orsini…"

"Seriously, Bissette," he said, dropping a light kiss on her mouth. "Just stay put. I'll be right back."

He returned with a package, dropped it in the rear seat

and pretended he didn't hear her questions. After a while she gave up.

"Nap time," he said, once they'd returned to the house.

That made her smile. Nap time had become an important part of their day, not that it actually involved napping. This time, however, after they made love—long, sweet, incredibly tender love—she fell asleep, curled against her lover's side.

And awoke, alone, in the bed.

She sat up, yawning. What time was it? It felt late. A glance at the clock proved that it was almost seven. Where was Falco? She loved waking with him in their bed. Not that this was actually "their" bed. It was so easy to fall into the fantasy, to let herself think that this would go on forever, that what he seemed to feel for her was…that it was real.

It wasn't, of course.

He was attracted to her. And concerned about her. But then, that was his job. Falco was her bodyguard. Her guardian. Yes, he'd developed some feeling for her, but it was sexual and that was okay because her feeling for him was the same and that was enough, that she'd gone from terror at the thought of a man touching her to wanting to be touched.

By Falco. Only by him. Always by him…

"Hello, sweetheart."

Elle looked up—and blinked at the apparition in the doorway. "Falco?"

He grinned. "Nobody else."

Nobody else, indeed. Her bodyguard wore a black tux with black silk lapels, black trousers that emphasized his narrow hips and long legs, a white shirt, a black bow tie…

He was beautiful.

"Am I dreaming?" she said, as he came toward her.

He laughed softly. "Close that gorgeous mouth, baby," he said, putting a finger lightly under her chin. "On second thought…" He bent down and kissed her, ran the tip of his tongue lightly over the sweet surface of her bottom lip. Then he straightened up and struck a pose. "Well? What do you think?"

Elle sat up against the pillows, the duvet drawn to her chin. If this was a dream, it was lovely.

"I think," she said, "that neither Walmart nor FedEx sells custom-made tuxes."

"Good conclusion."

"But?"

"But, FedEx is a wonderful thing, especially when a guy can call at least one brother with a key to his town house."

"You called your brother and had him send you a tux?" Elle laughed. "Because…?"

"Because, of course, we're going out to dinner."

"Out? You and me? But you said I had to keep a low profile."

"We're going to a very private place, baby."

"But—"

"Trust me."

Trust him? With all that she was, all she would ever be…

"Come on, Bissette. Get yourself all dressed up and meet me in the atrium."

Get dressed up. In what? Shorts? A T-shirt? Rubber thongs? He was more handsome than any actor in Hollywood, any male model in New York, and she was going to look like—

"Oh. One last thing." He smiled. "You might want to check the closet."

"For what?"

He cupped the back of her head, bent to her again and gave her a long, lingering kiss.

"What did I say, baby? Just trust me."

The instant the door shut after him, Elle scrambled from the bed and flung open the closet door….

"Oh," she whispered, "oh, Falco…"

A gown of amber silk hung before her. It was beautiful, the kind of thing she'd have picked for herself to wear for an evening with him. There were shoes, too, as delicate as if they'd been spun from gold. The only possible word for them was sexy. Narrow straps. Slender, spiked heels…

Tears rose in her eyes. Silly, to weep over something so sweet, so generous, so thoughtful…

Even more silly, to weep at the realization that she had fallen deeply, deeply in love with her bodyguard.

She showered.

Washed her hair.

Dried it, brushed it until it shone, then let it flow down her back. She put on mascara and lip gloss, which was twice the makeup she'd worn all week. Then she went back into the bedroom.

The gown lay across the bed. She didn't know how Falco had bought it; maybe his brothers had sent it. It was exquisite but there was a problem. She had no undergarments to go with it. The white cotton bras had straps that would show; the panties would be outlined under the softly clinging silk.

Elle shut her eyes.

She could wear it without underwear.

No. No, she couldn't. No underwear? Just the kiss of cool silk against her skin? The knowledge, all evening, that she was naked beneath it?

Her breath hitched.

She let the bath towel fall to the floor, picked up the gown and slipped it over her head. The silk slid down her body. It did, indeed, feel cool.

And she felt sexy. Wicked. Wonderfully, gloriously wicked. Wicked in a way that had nothing to do with Madison Avenue photo shoots or the artful fakery of Hollywood movie sets. She felt wicked the way a woman would surely want to feel for her lover.

She stepped into the sexy shoes and adjusted the straps. Ran her hands through her hair. Took a quick look at herself in the mirror and then, knowing she was a breath away from losing her courage, opened the door that led to the atrium and stepped outside.

Stepped into a world of glittering, shimmering candle-light.

There were dozens and dozens of candles. All shapes, all sizes, all glowing as brightly as stars.

A round table, draped in ivory linen and set with delicate china and gleaming sterling flatware, stood near the pool. There were candles on the table, too, elegant pink tapers on either side of a crystal vase overflowing with pink and white orchids. A serving cart laden with silver chafing dishes stood nearby; a bottle of champagne stood chilling in a silver wine cooler. Music played softly from hidden speakers, something soft and romantic and perfect....

But most perfect of all was Falco.

He stood beside the waterfall, watching her, and when she saw the look on his face, her heart soared.

"Elle," he said softly, "my beautiful, beautiful Elle."

His Elle. Yes. That was what she wanted to be. Smiling, she turned in a graceful circle.

"It's the gown. The shoes. How did you—"

"Magic," he said.

She laughed. "Magic, indeed."

He came slowly toward her, arms outstretched. "May I have this dance, Ms. Bissette?"

"Most assuredly, Mr. Orsini. My card is reserved for no one but you."

He gathered her to him. She looped her arms around his

neck. He made a sound deep in his throat. Had he realized she had nothing on beneath the gown? Surely he must have: her nipples were beaded against his chest, his hand lay at the very base of her spine. But he said nothing, simply held her as they began moving to the music.

"I was afraid the gown wouldn't do you justice," he said softly.

She leaned back in the circle of his arms and looked up at him. "The gown couldn't be more beautiful."

"Neither could you."

He meant it. She was, without question, the most beautiful woman he'd ever known. If only he'd bought her something else, something more to bring out the topaz fire of her eyes....

"Diamonds," he said. "Canary-yellow diamonds."

She laughed. "What?"

"It's what you need. One perfect heart-cut stone that would lie right here." He bent his head and kissed the hollow of her throat. He could feel her trembling against him, could feel her heart beating as fast as the wings of a hummingbird.

His heart lurched. He said her name, drew her closer and they began moving again, lost in the music and in each other.

"Falco." His name was the softest whisper on the still night air. "Falco," she said again, "Falco…"

He kissed her.

He wanted to take her inside, strip away the gown, bury himself deep inside her, but had planned this night for her. Nick, who had sent the tux, had started to ask questions but he'd cut them off with a terse, *I'll explain when I see you…*

Except, how could he explain what he didn't understand himself? When had this gone from being a mission to something else, something even more dangerous than the violence he knew he would eventually face? When had Elle become everything that mattered in his life?

What did all of that mean?

Falco cleared his throat, laced his fingers through hers and led her to the table. He seated her, took the chair across from hers and took the bottle of champagne from the silver bucket. The cork made a soft pop when he eased it free. He filled two flutes, gave Elle one.

"To this night," he said, touching his glass to hers.

"This perfect night," Elle said, smiling at him.

Her lover had thought of everything. Vichyssoise. Lobster. Asparagus. Chocolate mousse. Kona coffee with heavy cream, all as perfect as the night. At least, Elle assumed it was perfect. She couldn't taste anything. Her senses were all centered on him.

He poured the last of the champagne. Then he took her hand and brought it to his lips. "I wish we could have really gone out to dinner." He smiled. "Someplace where every man in the room would have cheerfully killed to change places with me."

She laughed. "What a wish!"

Falco flashed that gorgeous, macho grin. "What can I tell you, baby? Under all the smooth veneer, a cave is a guy's natural habitat."

"Well, for a caveman, you clean up pretty good." Elle looked around them, at the candles, the serving cart, and shook her head. "How did you manage all this?"

"I told you. Magic."

He was the magic. She came within a heartbeat of telling him that.

"Nobody ever…nobody in my entire life ever did anything like this for me."

He pushed the flowers aside, leaned forward and kissed her. "Part of me wishes someone had," he said softly. A smile of blatant male satisfaction angled over his mouth. "But the part that's living in that cave is glad I was the first."

She touched her hand to his face.

"You were the first for so many things," she whispered. "Especially about—about making love. I never…until you, I thought…I always thought—"

Her admission filled him with pleasure as well as pain. He hated knowing she'd feared sex…and yet, he exulted in the knowledge that he was the man who'd freed her of that fear.

"Hush," he said gruffly. "You don't have to explain."

"I didn't mean to embarrass you."

He turned his head and pressed a kiss to her palm.

"You could never embarrass me," he said roughly, "especially if you talk about what I make you feel."

Elle took a deep breath. "And me?" she murmured. "How do I make you feel?"

She waited for his answer, asking herself what had ever made her foolish enough to ask him such a question….

"As if you and I are alone on this planet," he said huskily. "As if nothing matters but us." He rose to his feet, drew her to hers, his eyes hot as fire. "As if the only thing under that gown is you."

Her heart leaped as he reached behind her for the zipper. He had undressed her many, many times over the past days and nights, but never like this. A week ago, this would have terrified her. Now, it sent waves of hot excitement through her blood.

The zipper opened. The thin straps of the gown fell from her shoulders and the slender column of amber silk drifted sensuously over her naked skin and became a discarded chrysalis at her feet.

Falco groaned. "Elle," he said, "God almighty, Elle…"

She trembled as his eyes swept over her. The look on his face… Her body's response was swift. She felt her breasts lift, her nipples bud. Heat pooled between her thighs.

"Falco," she whispered.

"Yes," he said, and he kissed her eyes, her mouth her throat.

Then he dropped to his knees and did what he had longed to do since the first time he'd made love to her, put his face against the soft curls that guarded her femininity.

Elle gasped. "No! You can't—"

His hands closed on her wrists as she reached out to stop him.

"I can," he said. "I have to."

Gently, he gently nuzzled her thighs apart. And kissed her.

Her cry tore through the night and he kissed her again, licked her, tasted her. Her orgasm raced through her, shattering her, turning her bones to liquid. He rose to his feet, scooped her into his arms, carried her to a *chaise longue* beside the pool and tore off his clothes. He entered her on one hard, deep thrust and she screamed as she came again. And again.

"Elle," he said, watching her face as he rode her, knowing that what he had told her the night they'd quarreled was the truth.

This wasn't sex.

It was far more than that.

It was—it was—

"Falco," she sobbed, and he flung back his head and let go.

They fell asleep wrapped around each other.

The night grew cool. A breeze swept in; the candles sputtered and went out. He woke with a start.

Elle was gone.

Falco shot to his feet...and saw her, at the far end of the atrium, wrapped in an oversized pool towel and staring blindly at the thin white line of surf beating against the sea.

He pulled on his trousers and went to her, slid his arms

around her and tried to pull her back against him but she stood stiff and unresponsive within his embrace.

"What's wrong, honey? Are you cold?"

"Falco. I have—I have to tell you—"

The words were heavy with meaning. A coldness that had nothing to do with the night went through him.

"You were right when you said I knew who's stalking me. I do know. I've known, all along." She swallowed, the sound audible in the silence of the atrium. "I just—I just don't know how to tell you…."

Falco held her closer. "Just tell me," he said softly. "Whatever it is, we'll deal with it together."

"His name is Willy Joe Johnson. He is…he was my stepfather." Elle drew a shuddering breath. "I told you that my real father died, remember? He was a coal miner. We lived in a little town in West Virginia and—and one day, there was an accident in the mine. My daddy and ten other miners didn't make it out."

Her voice had undergone a subtle change. It had taken on an accent, the softness of vowels he associated with small town girls from places where men risked their lives in the bowels of the earth.

"Go on," he said softly.

"My mama wasn't well. She hadn't been for a long time. With Papa gone, it was worse. We had no money. We got a little money from the union, but—but mostly, we lived on charity."

Falco shut his eyes, trying to block out the vision of a little girl with dark hair and topaz eyes, living on the kindness of strangers.

"Mama had a sister in Ohio. We moved there. But her sister had her own troubles. So we moved again, to Kentucky. Mama got a little better and she took a job but then she got sick again. We started going to this storefront church where there was a soup kitchen." She paused. "And a preacher."

Falco's gut knotted. Whatever came next would be dark and ugly. He wanted to turn Elle toward him, tell her she didn't have to say any more, but she did. What came next was at the heart of what had been happening to her.

"Willy Joe liked Mama. He seemed nice. And he said— he said he'd always wanted a little girl of his own. So, when I was thirteen, Mama married him. She did it for me. So I'd have food to eat and a roof over my head and—and—"

Falco turned her to him and set aside everything he knew about maintaining distance between himself and a client.

"You don't have to do this tonight, honey. It can wait until morning."

"No. It can't. It's waited too long as it is. You need to know. You have the right to know." Her voice broke. "I—I want you to know, do you see?"

So he let her talk.

She told him that she knew, almost right away, something was not right. Her stepfather barked at her mother, shouted at her. Even the house was unpleasant. It was dark and dirty. It had a bad feel to it.

And the walls were thin.

"They were very thin. I could hear what was happening in the next room, his and Mama's room, at night. Mama crying, Willy Joe grunting, but when I asked Mama, she said everything was fine. I knew it wasn't but I couldn't do anything to help her."

Falco cursed, swept Elle into his arms and carried her into the house. He sat down in an overstuffed living room chair and held her close.

"Mama got sick again. Real sick. And that was when—it was when Willy Joe started looking at me. Watching me. He'd brush against me as if it was an accident, come into the bathroom—the lock didn't work—and say he hadn't known I was in there. And then, one night, he came into my bedroom."

Falco said something ugly. Elle kept talking.

"He—he came every night after that. And he—he did things. But I wasn't there. Not really. I had this little stuffed animal my daddy had given me—"

"A toy cat," Falco said, because by now he knew, he knew.

Elle nodded. "I'd hold on to that cat and hold on to it, no matter what happened. I didn't scream, I didn't cry, I didn't tell anybody anything because Willy Joe told me what he'd do to Mama if I did."

And then, one morning, she said, her mother didn't wake up. The day of the funeral, her stepfather put his meaty hand on Elle's shoulder. He said that now, she really belonged to him.

He moved her into his room. Into the bed he'd shared with her mother. And that night—that night…

Elle began to sob. Falco went on holding her, rocking her, but his heart had become as cold as ice.

"I went to school the next morning," she said raggedly. "It was safer than staying home. But something must have showed because Miss Toner, my English teacher, asked if I was okay." She dragged in a breath. "'You can tell me, Ellie,' she said, and it was like a light coming on because she was right, I didn't have to protect Mama anymore. So I told her everything."

The rest of the story was straightforward. The teacher took her to the principal; the principal called the sheriff. Her stepfather was arrested. Elle, sixteen by then, was scheduled to testify at his trial but she didn't have to. Willy Joe pleaded guilty. He said only his God had the right to judge him.

"They sentenced him to fifty years and my teacher said he could never hurt me again…."

"But she was wrong," Falco said tonelessly. "When did he get out?"

"Six months ago. He found out where I lived. Sent me that—that horrible picture. He wrote to me. He told me I was going to pay for defying him and God. And then—and then, right before you showed up, he telephoned me…."

"Ah, baby. My sweet baby. Why didn't you go to the police?"

"Don't you see? Nobody knows what happened to me, Falco. Nobody but you. To have the whole world know—and it would be the whole world, this time—to have them stare and whisper, to have to live through the nightmare again…" She shuddered. "I was Ellie Janovic until Willy Joe was sentenced. The next day, I took a bus to New York. I became Elle Bissette. And I'm never going to be that other person again."

"Yes," he said, "yes, baby, I see."

And he did. Elle's scars went deep. She had survived a horrendous ordeal but if the media got hold of the story, she'd be victimized all over again.

He held her for hours, stroking her, comforting her, telling her that he would never let anything hurt her. Gradually, she stopped weeping and fell asleep, safe in his arms.

He wanted to hold her forever, but he couldn't. The monster had to be dealt with. To do that, he had to contain his anger. Hell, his rage. He had to formulate a plan.

Discipline. Self-control. Logic. Those had always been the bastions of his life.

Until he caught the bastard who'd done this to his Elle, he needed them more than ever.

CHAPTER TWELVE

A MAGICAL evening.

But everything changed, the next day. Everything including Falco.

He became...removed.

Elle couldn't think of another way to describe his behavior. He was there but he wasn't, not in the ways that mattered. There were no more long walks on the beach, no easy laughter, no drives along the back roads.

Something was wrong. The question was, what?

The change had been painfully abrupt. He'd been so wonderful that night. So tender, holding her in his arms until she slept, soothing her with whispers and caresses. At dawn, she'd felt him slip from the bed. She'd assumed he was going to use the bathroom but then she heard the rustle of cloth and she'd looked from under her lashes to see him putting on a T-shirt and a pair of denim cutoffs.

Come back to me, she'd almost said, but there'd been such caution in the way he moved that she'd remained silent. Silly, because he probably only wanted to make sure he didn't wake her, but when he left the room without at least dropping a light kiss on her lips, the first tendrils of doubt crept in. Had the things she told him changed the way he saw her?

No. That was crazy. He wasn't that kind of man, Elle told herself as she dressed and went looking for him. He wasn't in the kitchen or the atrium, he wasn't anywhere in the house. He was on the beach, making one call after another on his cell phone. When he was done, he stripped off his T-shirt and began exercising. One hundred push-ups. One hundred squats. And then what appeared to be a wild combination of kick-boxing and kung fu and tae kwon do.

After a while, sweat glistened on his body. A beautiful body she'd come to know with heart-stopping intimacy and yet—and yet, even his body seemed different. Beautiful, of course, but now she saw it could be a tool of violence.

She went back into the house and waited for him.

"Hey," she'd said as lightly as she could manage when he finally came in, "what's going on?"

"I've let things go," he'd answered. "Now I'm making up for it."

No kiss. No smile. Just those cool words as he headed for the shower.

By now, four days had gone by. Falco's morning workout routine became more intense. He seemed to be always on his phone. He spoke to her in short, clipped phrases. The most difficult thing to accept was that they didn't go to bed at the same time. They always had, since becoming lovers. Not anymore.

"You go ahead," Falco would say when it grew late. "I'll be a little while."

She fell asleep alone. Or didn't fall asleep, but it didn't matter. When he finally came to bed, he didn't touch her. Didn't hold her. And yet, during the darkest hours of the night, she'd awaken to his hard body against hers, to the drugging heat of his mouth, the skill of his hands moving over her and then the almost savage power of his possession.

No words. No whispers. Just that stunning, exciting joining of flesh to flesh.

In the morning, no matter how early she awoke, he was already gone.

At first, she wept. Not where he could see. Never that. Her heart ached; she longed for the man she'd come to know as Falco Orsini. Then tears gave way to anger. What was the point to self-pity? If she'd given in to that kind of defeatist behavior years ago, Elle Bissette would not exist.

What had created Elle Bissette was determination, guts and, yes, anger. Anger at her stepfather and then anger at herself for not getting on with her life. Anger was a strong, safe emotion. And by day four, it consumed her.

If Falco had a problem accepting the truth about her, why in hell had he insisted on hearing it? Why had he been so caring after she'd told him everything? Given time to think things over, had he regretted making love with a woman who, face it, Elle, was damaged goods?

Did he think he could have sex with her under cover of darkness and reject her when daylight came? If so, he had another think coming.

Elle glared out the window. She could see him down by the water, doing those ridiculous martial arts moves.

"Enough," she said through her teeth, "is enough."

She went out the door and strode toward him. If he heard her coming, he didn't show it. He went on grunting and straining, whirling around on one foot, kicking and jabbing. She snorted. He looked ridiculous….

Except, he didn't.

He looked graceful and almost dauntingly masculine, and for one desperate moment she almost flung herself into his arms to tell him that she wasn't angry or ticked off, she was in pain because he was breaking her heart…

"What do you want?"

She blinked. Falco stood glaring at her, his hands on his hips.

"Elle. If you have something to say, spit it out. I'm busy here."

Elle narrowed her eyes and slapped her hands on her hips, mimicking his posture without realizing it.

"I want to know what's going on."

"I'm working out. That's what's going on."

"You know what I mean. Where have you been all week?"

He stared at her. She thought she saw awareness in his eyes, but then he grabbed a towel and rubbed it over his face. When he looked at her again, his eyes were blank.

"I've been doing what I should have been doing from the start. A bodyguard's not much use if he's not in shape."

"And this occurred to you because…?"

Falco struggled to remain unmoved. She was angry. Her color was high. Her voice was sharp. She'd obviously tumbled out of bed and put herself together in a rush because her hair was tangled and she hadn't bothered with a bra; he could see the pout of her nipples against the thin cotton of her tank top.

She was, in other words, mouth-wateringly delicious. She always was.

Going to bed without enfolding her in his arms each night was agony. Leaving her each morning was just as tough. He didn't think about it so much during the day because he was busy from morning until night, getting back in shape, talking with the guy who'd gotten him the gun here in Maui and another guy he knew and trusted back in L.A., planning every move a dozen times over because if he made a mistake, his Elle was the one who would pay.

Even so, there'd been times the last few days she'd walked by him and he'd wanted to grab her. Haul her into his arms.

Tell her he was doing this for her, that this was the only way he knew to pull off something so dangerous, that it was the most important thing he'd ever undertaken because of what he felt for her.

He didn't, of course.

Control. Containment. Discipline. Making plans and reviewing them until they were part of him. It had to be handled like this.

That he lost all that control and containment and discipline in the dark hours of the night, that he was too damned weak to keep from turning to her, taking her in his arms, seeking comfort in her warmth, her silkiness, her almost pagan response to him...

That he permitted that to happen was wrong.

How could he prepare for what came next unless he kept his mind and body separate? And that was the problem. He couldn't seem to keep them separate anymore. Something inside him had changed; he didn't just want to touch Elle, he wanted to think about her. All the time. To make her part of him. To tell her—to tell her that he—that he—

His cell phone beeped. Falco almost groaned with relief as he snatched it from his pocket and shot a look at it. It was the guy from L.A.

"Yes?"

"Bingo," the guy said. "My contact at the *L.A. Times* came through. The article reads..." There was the rustle of paper. "It reads, 'Everybody can stop wondering why Elle Bissette walked off the set. She's been spotted canoodling with her latest at a private estate off Paradise Road on the beach at Maui.' Plus, his wife works for *Entertainment Tonight*. She got the same item online and on TV yesterday."

"Perfect. And the rest?"

"Well, you already know I located your man three days back, and that I've been on him ever since."

Falco looked at Elle, then swung away from her. "And?"

"And, he's getting ready to make his move. In fact, I'm standing a few feet away from him right now. He bought a ticket to Maui at the American Airlines counter. His flight's due to land at midnight, your time."

Falco nodded. "Good work," he said softly. "And Rick? Thanks."

"*De nada*, dude. Feels like old times, right?"

"Right." Falco disconnected, hit a speed dial button. Jack, the guy in Maui, picked up on the first ring.

"Yeah?"

"Time to rock and roll, Jack."

"I'm ready, man. I'll be there in an hour."

Falco closed his phone and turned to Elle. This would be the hardest part of all.

"Who," she said coldly, "was that?"

"A couple of friends." He paused. "I need their help so I can take care of your problem."

Elle saw something cold and primitive flicker in his eyes. All her anger drained away.

"Oh, God," she whispered, "Falco—"

"Your stalker is on his way here. You and I both know what he intends to do." A muscle tightened in his jaw. "Except, things won't go exactly the way he figures."

"Falco." Elle took a step toward him. "What are you saying?"

He tucked his phone in his pocket, draped the towel around his neck, grabbed his shirt and started for the house. Elle had to run to keep up.

"Answer me," she said. "What are you going to do?"

"Whatever needs doing."

"No!" She caught his arm, swung in front of him. "He'll kill you!"

Falco laughed. Elle shook her head.

"Falco. Please. Call the police."

"You gave me good reasons why the police shouldn't get involved in this," he said, shaking her off and continuing towards the house.

"I've changed my mind. If you get hurt—"

"I won't."

"Dammit, nobody's immortal!"

He stopped and swung toward her again. "I told you. I'm not going to get hurt."

"But—but if—if you should…" Her eyes searched his. "I'd be—I'd be—"

"What?" he said in a low voice.

"I'd be—" She stared at him. Heartbroken, she thought. Devastated. Lost for the rest of my life because I love you, love you—

Did the words spill from her lips? All she knew was that Falco cursed, grabbed her by the shoulders, hauled her to him and took her mouth in a bruising kiss. Elle sobbed his name, all but jumped into his arms, wrapped her arms and legs around him and kissed him back. His hands snaked under her tank top; he said something she couldn't understand as he tore it from her. Her shorts and panties followed.

Naked, she moaned his name as he backed her against the house, fumbled at his fly and then he thrust into her, hard, deep, all of him hot and rigid within her wet, welcoming heat. She screamed with pleasure, screamed again and again until he had emptied himself into her. He held her for a long moment, her face against his throat, his arms tight around her. Then, slowly, he lowered her to her feet.

"I'm not going to let you do this," she said in a shaky whisper. "You don't know what he's like. He'll—"

"I know precisely what he's like." Falco scooped up her clothing and handed it to her. He didn't want to see her naked like this. It made him want to take her in his arms and hold her to his heart and there wasn't a way in hell he was going to let that happen. "Put your clothes on," he said roughly.

Color swept into her face but, she went right on facing him, the clothes held to her breasts.

"Falco. I beg you. Listen to me—"

"Do you hear me, dammit? Go inside. Get dressed. Pack. There'll be someone here soon to fly you to Los Angeles."

"Fly me...? No! I won't go. If you're going to be so—so pigheaded, I'll stay. I'm not leaving you."

His mouth twisted as he moved past her, into the coolness of the house.

"I'm not giving you a choice, Bissette."

"Wait a minute. Wait just one damned minute!" Elle rushed after him, grabbed his arm. Tears of anger and frustration streaked her face. Looking at her made his throat constrict.

"I love you," she said. "Do you understand? I love you! I'm not going to let you do this. I love you. And you—and you love—"

His heart turned over. She was right about part of that. He loved her. Why deny the truth to himself? He loved her with every fiber of his being and that made it all the more imperative to get her out of here. He could not do what he had to do if he worried about her stepfather somehow getting past him and putting his filthy hands on her.

There was only one way to make sure she left, and he took it.

"You're wrong," he said, fighting to keep his emotions from showing. "You don't love me."

"Dammit, Orsini, do not tell me what—"

"And I sure as hell don't love you. You're beautiful and desirable and sexy but wanting you isn't loving you."

Her face paled. "Falco. You don't mean—"

"You needed a knight errant. And there I was, riding in to save you."

Elle shook her head. "That's not how it was. It was more than that. It was—"

"It was sex," he said bluntly. "Great sex." She tried to look away from him. He caught hold of her and forced her to meet his cool gaze. "Yeah, we made love. But making love isn't the same as being in love."

A moan escaped her lips. He knew he would never forget this moment just as he knew that at least part of what he'd told her was true. She didn't love him. For all her sophistication, his Elle was an innocent. She'd never loved a man, never lain in a man's arms, and she'd damned well never had a man do battle to save her.

Add it all up, she was confusing gratitude with love. He knew it and, once she got a little distance from what had happened, so would she.

"So…" She paused. "So, you were just doing your job?"

"And it isn't over."

She nodded. "But we are," she whispered.

Falco shrugged his shoulders. "You've got it."

She took a step back. Her nose was running; she swiped at it with the clothing balled in her hand. She had forgotten she was naked and he let his eyes sweep over her one last time.

She thought she saw something flash in those eyes…until he simply turned and walked away.

Then she knew, for sure, what they'd had—what she'd let herself believe they'd had—was finished.

CHAPTER THIRTEEN

JACK, THE Maui guy, showed up.

Falco introduced him to Elle. Elle said nothing. Not to his old pal, not to him. Well, sure. What was there left to say after you'd said it all?

Elle got into Jack's car and they left for the airport. Falco had chartered a plane to take them to L.A. He watched until the car was just a spot of dust. His heart was heavy but he knew Elle would be safe. Back in the day, he and Jack had trusted each other with their lives. They still did.

It was time to prepare for Willy Joe Johnson's arrival.

He checked the house, its perimeter, touched up a couple of refinements he'd made to the security system. An hour later, Rick, the L.A. guy, phoned. Willy Joe's plane had taken off on time. Elle's stepfather was on his way to Maui.

Falco ate a light meal. Checked his weapon. He looked at his watch, set it for midnight, lay down on a bed—not the one he'd shared with Elle—and slept. He woke a minute before the watch beeped, threw cold water on his face, went into the dark living room and settled in to wait.

Jack phoned. He and Elle were in L.A., in the suite Falco had reserved at the Four Seasons. Everything was fine, except Elle still wasn't talking to him.

That made Falco smile. What a tough lady she was.

Midnight came and went…one a.m., two a.m. Still nothing. Time was dragging.

He thought back over the last few days, thought about Elle. Sending her away had been the right thing, the only thing. She'd fallen in love with the idea of love, not with him.

And he—he would forget. The taste of her mouth. The warmth of her in his arms. The exquisite feel of her closing around him as they'd made love for the very last time.

That had been wrong. Terribly wrong. He'd known that even as he'd slipped deep inside her, but having her that one last time had been as vital as drawing breath….

The lights on the silent alarm console blinked to life. Falco felt his pulse start to race.

Elle's stepfather had arrived.

In the end, much of Falco's planning hadn't been worth a damn.

He'd expected a stealthy attack. The rear door. The front door. The door to the atrium.

Instead, there was a horrendous crash.

Johnson, evidently not given to subtlety, had smashed his way into the atrium. Moonlight illuminated him, six feet six inches of lard laid over prison-honed muscle.

He had a knife in his hand.

"Where is she?" Willy Joe shouted. "Where is that heathen bitch whose lies sent me to prison?"

Falco stepped into the atrium, gun drawn.

"She's where you can't hurt her," he said in a low, hard voice. "You're never going to hurt her again."

Willy Joe spat on the terrazzo floor. "She lured me to her. Seduced me. She's a whore, just like her mama." He curved his body forward, spread his feet apart. It was the stance of a man who knew how to use the silvery blade he held. "Now she's your whore, Orsini. But not for long. I'm going to kill you and then I'll kill her." He smiled, the smile of a maniac. "Get ready to meet your maker."

Willy Joe took a shuffling step forward. All Falco had to do was pull the trigger and a bullet traveling at better than 1,000 feet per second would stop this hulking mountain of vile flesh.

Instead, he tossed the gun aside.

He had no knife. No other weapon. What he had was the hot, blazing rage a man can only feel when the woman he loves has been violated.

"Come on and try it, you son of a bitch," he growled, and Willy Joe cackled and came at him.

The stalker was as big as a mountain but Falco was fast. And he was all muscle, no fat laid over it. He lunged to the left, feinted to the right and struck out. The first blow staggered Willy Joe but he shook it off, rushed Falco again and closed his massive arms around him. They wrestled. Struggled. Fell to the glass-strewn floor and rolled. Suddenly, the knife was driving down toward Falco's throat.

"Whore-master," Willy Joe shouted, but all Falco could hear was the sound of Elle weeping, the night she'd told him what she'd endured.

Falco roared. Grabbed his attacker's wrist. Slowly, slowly, grunting with the effort, he forced the hand holding the knife backward, toward Willy Joe.

The blade sank in.

Willy Joe gasped, then froze. And rolled onto his back, dead.

Falco shook his head to clear it, got to his knees and looked down at the stalker.

"Give my regards to the devil," he said hoarsely.

Then he staggered to his feet and took out his cell phone, which was when he realized he'd been cut. It didn't matter.

The monster who had caused the woman he loved years and years of pain was no more.

The police arrived, then a crime scene crew and a pair of detectives.

The detective in charge took Falco's statement, took notes, poked Willy Joe's body with the shiny toe of one black brogue.

"Mean SOB," his partner said. "Checked him on the computer soon as we got the call from the local guys."

Falco nodded. The EMTs had cleaned his wounds. He needed stitches but that could wait.

"So, you were staying here, on vacation, and this mother turned up from out of nowhere?"

Falco nodded again. "He must have figured the house was empty and filled with expensive stuff he could steal."

"Not his M.O.," the first detective said. "Guy was arrested and did time years ago for raping a kid."

"Well," Falco said, "I guess he decided to try something different."

"And you were here, alone. Big place, for one man."

Falco forced a smile. "I had some company for a couple of days," he said, knowing that if they checked, the best anybody would do was give a vague description of a woman.

The second detective cleared his throat. "You know, I mentioned you to my captain, Orsini. Says he knew you, back a ways in the Middle East. Knew of you, anyway. Says you were involved in some nasty stuff, says it's a damned good thing Johnson happened to choose this place to rob, that he'd surely have killed anybody else who'd tried to stop him."

Falco shrugged. "The luck of the draw."

The detectives looked at each other. "Yeah," the one in charge said with a quick smile, "that's what it must have been. The luck of the draw."

* * *

Elle read about it in an L.A. newspaper.

She knew things had gone the way Falco had intended because his friend, Jack, got a call from Falco, smiled and told her she could leave the hotel anytime. He wouldn't say more than that.

It was a small article, just a few lines. An ex-convict had broken into a house on Maui and attacked the vacationer staying there. The vacationer had killed him. No names mentioned; it wasn't an important enough news item for that.

A clear case of self-defense, said the police, but it would be up to the district attorney to make the final decision.

Elle put the paper down. Her hands were trembling.

Her tormenter was dead. Her lover had killed him. The man she loved—because, yes, she loved Falco and always would, despite the fact that he didn't love her—the man she loved had risked his life, even his freedom, for her.

And what had she done for him except run away?

He'd forced her to leave but the truth was, she could have bolted once his friend got her to the airport. What would the man have done about it? Tie her up? Drag her, kicking and screaming, onto the waiting chartered plane? Not hardly.

She had let Falco drive her away because she couldn't bear the thought that he didn't love her, that he would never love her, that she had been a job and sex and nothing more.

But what about all the rest?

He had brought her out of a lifetime of darkness. He had shown her that sex, that making love, could be joyful. He was her knight and he'd slain the dragon—and she'd abandoned him.

What if the D.A. didn't agree with the police? What if he brought Falco up on charges? Surely there could be consequences. Assault? Manslaughter? Murder?

Tears rose in her eyes. All her life, all the past months, she had thought only of herself. Now, it was time to think of someone else. The one man she would always love.

Her dark knight. Her Falco.

Falco sat in his office in the Orsini Brothers building in downtown Manhattan.

He had a stack of papers on his desk; he knew his e-mail box was stuffed. He'd blown off a meeting this morning and he was in no mood for one scheduled for this afternoon, either.

He leaned forward, hit the button on his intercom.

"Yes sir, Mr. Orsini?"

Falco sighed. His P.A. was new. He'd told her, a dozen times, to call him Falco.

"Cancel my three o'clock, please. Make it for next week."

As if anything would change by next week. As if anything would ever change, he thought, and tilted back his chair.

All he could think about was Elle.

He missed her. He ached for her. He thought of her each morning when he woke up, thought of her last thing at night, dreamed of her.

His brothers sensed something was up. They were about as subtle as elephants in a Victorian parlor. He knew they'd been talking about him. Last night, they'd badgered him into having beer and burgers at The Bar, the place they owned in SoHo. He hadn't wanted to go. The last thing he was in the mood for was fun and games but he'd figured it was easier to agree and then cut out early.

Not early enough, as it had turned out. The burgers hadn't even arrived when Raffaele flashed a phony smile and said, "So, Falco, how're things going?"

"They're going fine," he'd replied.

"Because," Dante had said, "well, you know, if anything's wrong…"

"Why would anything be wrong?" he'd said.

He'd changed the subject, talked some inane nonsense about baseball and they'd let him do it but sooner or later, they'd start pushing. And when they did—

"Falco?"

He looked up. Raffaele, Dante and Nicolo had cracked the door. They were peering in at him and, dammit, they had that look, the look they all got, him included, when they were worried about each other.

Well, hell. He didn't want anyone worrying about him.

"Hey, guys," he said, flashing a big smile, "I'd love to hang around and talk but—"

The three of them stepped into his office. Rafe shut the door.

"But what?" Dante said.

"But, I have a three o'clock appointment. And—"

"The hell you do," Rafe said. "You just cancelled."

Falco sighed. "That new P.A. is never going to work out."

Nick cleared his throat. "What's going on? And don't tell us nothing's going on. We know that's not true."

Falco looked from one of his brothers to the other. For one wild second, he almost blurted it out, almost said, *I met the only woman I'll ever love and I destroyed any possible hope she might have cared for me—*

"Whatever it is," he said coolly, "I don't need the Three Musketeers busting into my life."

"Think of us more as the Spanish Inquisition." Rafe grinned. "We have ways of making you talk."

Falco shoved back his chair and rose to his feet. "Okay, gentlemen, that's it. This meeting is—"

"Do your amazingly high spirits have anything to do with that errand our old man laid on you?"

Falco's eyes narrowed. "What'd you do, Nick? Put your ear to the door?"

Nick grinned. "Hey, I wasn't even there. I got tired of waiting and I took off."

"Yeah, well, good for you. Now, if you'll all excuse me—"

"Dammit, Falco," Dante said, "what's happening with you?"

Falco glared at his brothers. "I'll tell you what's happening with me," he snarled. "I met a woman, okay? And I—I got involved. And I told her I didn't give a damn for her. And—and, hell, it was a lie."

His brothers looked at each other. They were almost as shocked as Falco by his admission.

"So," Rafe said, "so, ah, go tell her. Tell her you—"

The intercom buzzed. Falco slapped the talk button. "Dammit," he roared, "what do you want?"

"I just…someone is here to see you, Mr. Orsini. Sir. I told her you were busy but—"

"But," Elle said as she opened the door and stepped into the office, "I told her I'd only take a minute of your time."

Falco blinked. "Elle?"

She nodded, looked around and bit lightly into her bottom lip. "You must be Falco's brothers."

Rafe and Nick and Dante nodded. Introduced themselves. Shook her hand. Looked at Falco, waited for him to say something…

"Go away," he said, and the three of them rushed for the door and shut it behind them.

"Elle." Falco could feel his heart racing. "You look—you look wonderful."

"Thank you. I guess I should have called first…"

"No," he said quickly, "no, I'm—I'm glad to see you."

Elle's mouth had gone dry. This was her Falco. The man

she adored. She wanted to run into his arms but that wasn't why she'd come here.

And it wasn't what he wanted.

She swallowed hard. "I read about—about what happened."

Hell, Falco thought, she'd hated Johnson but who knew how she felt now, knowing that he had killed him.

"The paper didn't say much, just that Willy Joe—that he broke in and—"

"We scuffled. I lucked out."

"He could have killed you!"

"No way," he said with a smile meant to be reassuring, "you know what they say about guys who were born to be hung."

"Falco." Her eyes blurred. She came toward him, lightly touched the small scar above his eyebrow. "Oh," she whispered, "did he—did he—"

"It's nothing." But the cool touch of her hand was almost more than he could bear. He caught her hand and laced his fingers through hers. God, he wanted to take her in his arms…

"The paper said that the police called it self-defense but that the final decision would be up to the district attorney."

"Right. It always is. And—"

"And," Elle said, hurrying the words together, "and if he decided it wasn't, you'll have to stand trial."

"No. I mean, yes, but—"

"I won't let that happen! I'm going to fly to Maui."

"What?"

"I said, I'm going to Maui. I'll tell the D.A. exactly what happened. How—how Willy Joe abused me. How he was sentenced to prison because of me and how he hated me for it and stalked me and—and—"

Falco felt the first flutter of hope. "Why would you do that?" he said softly.

"Because—because it's the right thing to do. I can't let you go to prison because of me."

He reached out and touched her hair. He couldn't help it. The need to stroke those dark strands one last time was too strong.

"I won't go to prison, honey. The D.A. reached a decision a couple of days ago. There won't be any charges."

Elle let out her breath. "Oh, I'm so glad!"

"You'd have done that, for me? Gone to the D.A.? Let your story go public?"

She nodded.

"Because?"

"I told you. It's the right thing to—"

Falco had lived his life taking risks. Now, he took the greatest risk of all.

"Tell me the truth," he said huskily. "Why would you do all that for me?" She didn't answer and he took her in his arms. "Is it because you love me, baby? Because you love me the way I love you?"

Tears spilled from her eyes. "Do you mean it? That you love me? Because I love you, Falco, I adore you. And—and I'd do anything for you, my knight, anything, anything—"

He kissed her. She gave a little cry, rose on her toes and wrapped her arms around his neck.

"Are you sure?" she said, against his lips. "Please be sure!"

"I love you with all my heart," he said huskily. "I love Ellie Janovic and I love Elle Bissette. With all my heart, all my soul. I'll love you until the end of time. Don't you know that by now?"

Elle made a sound that was half laugh, half sob. "You said you didn't. And you said I didn't love you. You said—"

"Hush," Falco said, and kissed her again. "I said a lot of things that day, every one a lie." He smoothed his thumbs over her cheekbones, felt the warmth of her tears against his skin.

"I loved you then. I love you now. I was just afraid you'd fallen for the man you thought I was—"

"I did. I fell for my knight in shining armor."

"I'm no knight, honey. I'm a lot of things but not that."

Elle smiled. "How little you know, Orsini. Of course you're a knight. My knight. And you always will be."

He smiled back at her. "You are one tough broad, Bissette. There's no arguing with you when you're sure you're right, is there?"

"Not about this," she said. "Never about this."

Falco drew her closer. "Still, there are things about me you don't know."

"For instance."

"For instance, your knight's old man is a crime boss."

"You already mentioned that." Elle laid a light kiss on Falco's lips. "So it's a good thing I'm not in love with your old man. What else?"

"Well," he said, straight-faced, "the other thing is even worse. I'm not a bodyguard."

"I sort of figured that when I looked in the Manhattan directory and found the listing for Orsini Brothers."

"Yeah. I'm an investor, along with those three idiots who just stumbled out the door."

"An investor." She smiled. "You're right. Considering everything, that might be even worse." She kissed him again. "But I'm willing to survive it if you can."

"Elle." Falco's expression grew serious. "Elle, will you marry me?"

Her eyes filled with happy tears. "Just try and stop me, Orsini," she said, and Falco reached past her, locked the door and kissed her.

EPILOGUE

THEY were married in the same little church in Greenwich Village that had so recently been the setting for Dante's and Rafe's weddings. Mercifully, no police cars were parked outside and only one photographer showed up. He beat a quick retreat after the Orsini brothers had a little talk with him.

Elle wore ivory silk; she carried a trailing bouquet of white orchids and wore her new mother-in-law's wedding veil, which made Sofia beam with delight. A heart-shaped canary-yellow diamond glittered in the hollow of her throat; another adorned the ring finger of her left hand.

Falco was gorgeous in the same tux he'd worn on what Elle called their first date, back in Hawaii. Isabella, Anna, Chiara and Gabriella were her bridesmaids, all of them beautiful in gowns of pink silk. Her new brothers-in-law kissed her and told her how happy they were to have her in their family.

The reception was held in the conservatory of the Orsini mansion. Everyone laughed, drank champagne, ate lobster and caviar and even managed bites of the huge wedding cake.

By late afternoon, things were getting quiet.

The bride and groom slipped away. They were going to Hawaii, though not to Maui, on their honeymoon. Dante and Gaby left with their son, Daniel, asleep in his daddy's arms.

Rafe and Chiara left, too. Chiara was pregnant, glowing with happiness, as was Rafe.

Nicolo kissed his mother goodbye, avoided his father as he'd done all day. Avoiding Cesare was habit; he didn't like the Don any more than his brothers did and besides, Nick was very aware of the fact that he had, thus far, avoided the talk Cesare had wanted to have with him a few months ago on the day Dante and Gabriella had married.

He and Falco had both been told their father wanted to see them. Falco had gone in first, Nick had waited outside for a few minutes and then he'd though, *Eff this*, which was exactly what he'd said to Felix, his father's *capo*, had put out a hand to stop him from leaving.

"I am not one of the Don's soldiers," Nick had said coldly. "He wants to see me, let him call and make an appointment."

But there'd been no call and Nick had figured he'd escaped his father's latest "after I'm dead" speech.

"Nicolo."

Nick, halfway to the front door of the big house, groaned. He took a deep breath and turned around.

"Father," he said politely.

"We must talk."

"I have an appointment. And you and I have nothing to talk about."

Cesare smiled around the fat, unlit Havana cigar clutched between his teeth.

"But we do. Besides, you owe me a few minutes. Did you think I had forgotten how you slipped out the last time?"

"I didn't 'slip out', Father, I just got tired of cooling my heels like one of your men."

"Exactly. You are not one of my men, you are my son. Surely, you will give me the courtesy of a chat just as your three brothers have done before you."

Nick's jaw tightened. His father was right. Dante, Raffaele and Falco had all gone through the wringer. It was his turn now, and he wasn't a man to walk away from a responsibility.

"Five minutes," he said brusquely. "That's it."

"Of course, Nicolo," Cesare said smoothly. "In my study, *per favore*. Yes?"

Nick strode toward the dark, overfurnished room from which Cesare ruled his empire.

"Whatever speech you've prepared, Father, had better be good."

The Don's *capo*, silent as a cat, stepped out of the shadows. Cesare motioned him aside and followed his son into the study.

"I assure you, Nicolo," he said as he shut the door, "it is."

HARLEQUIN *Presents*

Coming Next Month

from **Harlequin Presents® EXTRA.** Available November 9, 2010.

Coming Next Month

from **Harlequin Presents®.** Available November 23, 2010.

LARGER-PRINT BOOKS!

Harlequin Presents

PASSION GUARANTEED SEDUCTION

GET 2 FREE LARGER-PRINT NOVELS PLUS 2 FREE GIFTS!

YES! Please send me 2 FREE LARGER-PRINT Harlequin Presents® novels and my 2 FREE gifts (gifts are worth about $10). After receiving them, if I don't wish to receive any more books, I can return the shipping statement marked "cancel". If I don't cancel, I will receive 6 brand-new novels every month and be billed just $4.55 per book in the U.S. or $5.24 per book in Canada. That's a saving of at least 13% off the cover price! It's quite a bargain! Shipping and handling is just 50¢ per book.* I understand that accepting the 2 free books and gifts places me under no obligation to buy anything. I can always return a shipment and cancel at any time. Even if I never buy another book, the two free books and gifts are mine to keep forever.

176/376 HDN E5NG

Name	(PLEASE PRINT)	
Address		Apt. #
City	State/Prov.	Zip/Postal Code

Signature (if under 18, a parent or guardian must sign)

Mail to the **Harlequin Reader Service:**
IN U.S.A.: P.O. Box 1867, Buffalo, NY 14240-1867
IN CANADA: P.O. Box 609, Fort Erie, Ontario L2A 5X3

Not valid for current subscribers to Harlequin Presents Larger-Print books.

**Are you a subscriber to Harlequin Presents books
and want to receive the larger-print edition?
Call 1-800-873-8635 today!**

* Terms and prices subject to change without notice. Prices do not include applicable taxes. Sales tax applicable in N.Y. Canadian residents will be charged applicable provincial taxes and GST. Offer not valid in Quebec. This offer is limited to one order per household. All orders subject to approval. Credit or debit balances in a customer's account(s) may be offset by any other outstanding balance owed by or to the customer. Please allow 4 to 6 weeks for delivery. Offer available while quantities last.

Your Privacy: Harlequin Books is committed to protecting your privacy. Our Privacy Policy is available online at www.eHarlequin.com or upon request from the Reader Service. From time to time we make our lists of customers available to reputable third parties who may have a product or service of interest to you. If you would prefer we not share your name and address, please check here. ☐

Help us get it right—We strive for accurate, respectful and relevant communications. To clarify or modify your communication preferences, visit us at www.ReaderService.com/consumerschoice.

HPLP10R

HARLEQUIN®

A Romance

FOR EVERY MOOD™

Spotlight on

Classic

Quintessential, modern love stories
that are romance at its finest.

See the next page
to enjoy a sneak peek from
the Harlequin® Romance series.

Introducing DADDY BY CHRISTMAS by Patricia Thayer.

MIA caught sight of Jarrett when he walked into the open lobby. It was hard not to notice the man. In a charcoal business suit with a crisp white shirt and striped tie covered by a dark trench coat, he looked more Wall Street than small-town Colorado.

Mia couldn't blame him for keeping his distance. He was probably tired of taking care of her.

Besides, why would a man like Jarrett McKane be interested in her? Why would he want to take on a woman expecting a baby? Yet he'd done so many things for her. He'd been there when she'd needed him most. How could she not care about a man like that?

Heart pounding in her ears, she walked up behind him. Jarrett turned to face her. "Did you get enough sleep last night?"

"Yes, thanks to you," she said, wondering if he'd thought about their kiss. Her gaze went to his mouth, then she quickly glanced away. "And thank you for not bringing up my meltdown."

Jarrett couldn't stop looking at Mia. Blue was definitely her color, bringing out the richness of her eyes.

"What meltdown?" he said, trying hard to focus on what she was saying. "You were just exhausted from lack of sleep and worried about your baby."

He couldn't help remembering how, during the night, he'd kept going in to watch her sleep. How strange was that? "I hope you got enough rest."

She nodded. "Plenty. And you're a good neighbor for

coming to my rescue."

He tensed. Neighbor? *What neighbor kisses you like I did?* "That's me, just the full-service landlord," he said, trying to keep the sarcasm out of his voice. He started to leave, but she put her hand on his arm.

"Jarrett, what I meant was you went beyond helping me." Her eyes searched his face. "I've asked far too much of you."

"Did you hear me complain?"

She shook her head. "You should. I feel like I've taken advantage."

"Like I said, I haven't minded."

"And I'm grateful for everything…"

Grasping her hand on his arm, Jarrett leaned forward. The memory of last night's kiss had him aching for another. "I didn't do it for your gratitude, Mia."

Gorgeous tycoon Jarrett McKane has never believed in Christmas—but he can't help being drawn to soon-to-be-mom Mia Saunders! Christmases past were spent alone…and now Jarrett may just have a fairy-tale ending for all his Christmases future!

*Available December 2010,
only from Harlequin® Romance®.*

HREXP1210

Silhouette Desire

USA TODAY bestselling authors

MAUREEN CHILD

and

SANDRA HYATT

UNDER THE MILLIONAIRE'S MISTLETOE

Just when these leading men thought they had it all figured out, they quickly learn their hearts have made other plans. Two passionate stories about love, longing and the infinite possibilities of kissing under the mistletoe.

Available December wherever you buy books.

Always Powerful, Passionate and Provocative.

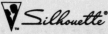

HARLEQUIN *Presents*®

Bestselling Harlequin Presents® author

Julia James

brings you her most powerful book yet…

FORBIDDEN OR
FOR BEDDING?

The shamed mistress…

Guy de Rochemont's name is a byword for wealth
and power—and now his duty is to wed.

Alexa Harcourt knows she can never be anything
more than *The de Rochemont Mistress*.

But Alexa—the one woman Guy wants—is also
the one woman whose reputation
forbids him to take her as his wife….

**Available from Harlequin Presents
December 2010**